A DARING ESCAPE

I was thirteen—no, fourteen—years old and I was in prison because I played a practical joke on the rich neighbor who bought my grampa's farm. My grampa is in a nursing home now, but it used to be, when things were bad at home, I could escape to Grampa's. That's why I hated Mr. DiAngelo so much. He was the snooty guy who bought Grampa's farm, tore the house down, then build a mansion there so he could show off how much money he had. One day, he even kicked me and my friends off his property. So I played a joke on the a-hole, only the joke went sour and his little boy died . . . .

For a minute there, the memories stopped. It was like hitting a wall. Everything stopped for me when I thought back on what I done. Which is why I tried not to think back on it. What good did it do? I couldn't undo the past.

I went to prison for my crime, but now I needed to get home, so I escaped in a garbage truck, which is how I came to be squashed beneath a ton of garbage.

The sound of a distant siren pierced the air. I knew if I didn't crawl out of that garbage and disappear, I'd be right back where I came from with even more time ahead of me.

OTHER BOOKS YOU MAY ENJOY

THE
JOURNEY
BACK

PRISCILLA CUMMINGS

PUFFIN BOOKS
An Imprint of Penguin Group (USA) Inc.

PUFFIN BOOKS
An imprint of Penguin Young Readers Group
Published by the Penguin Group
Penguin Group (USA) Inc.
375 Hudson Street
New York, New York 10014, U.S.A.

USA / Canada / UK / Ireland / Australia /
New Zealand / India / South Africa / China
Penguin Books Ltd, Registered Offices: 80 Strand, London WC2R 0RL, England

For more information about the Penguin Group visit www.penguin.com

First published in the United States of America by Dutton Children's Books,
an imprint of Penguin Young Readers Group, 2012
Published by Puffin Books, an imprint of Penguin Young Readers Group, 2013

Permission for quote on pages 125–126 from "Walking on a Wire": from Voyager
Passport Book C, Fluency Reader, Book 2, Adventures 5–8, Copyright 2008.
Map on pages vi–vii courtesy of the National Park Service.

THE LIBRARY OF CONGRESS HAS CATALOGED THE DUTTON CHILDREN'S BOOK EDITION AS FOLLOWS:
Cummings, Priscilla, 1951–
The journey back / Priscilla Cummings.
Companion to: Red kayak
p. cm.
978-0-525-42362-1 (hc)
Summary: After breaking out of juvenile detention, fourteen-year-old Digger
stops his trek across Maryland at a campground where he recovers from
injuries, cares for little Luke, works with smart and pretty Nora, and begins to
understand how his behavior and choices shape his life.
[1. Fugitives from justice—Fiction. 2. Conduct of life—Fiction. 3. Coming of
age—Fiction. 4. Camping—Fiction. 5. Voyages and travels—Fiction. 6. Juvenile
detention homes—Fiction.]
I. Title
PZ7.C9149 Jou 2012 [Fic]—dc23 2012003818

Puffin Books ISBN 978-0-14-242290-8

Printed in the United States of America

3 5 7 9 10 8 6 4 2

For John

———————————

CHESAPEAKE AND OHIO CANAL
NATIONAL HISTORICAL PARK MAP

(continues on next page)

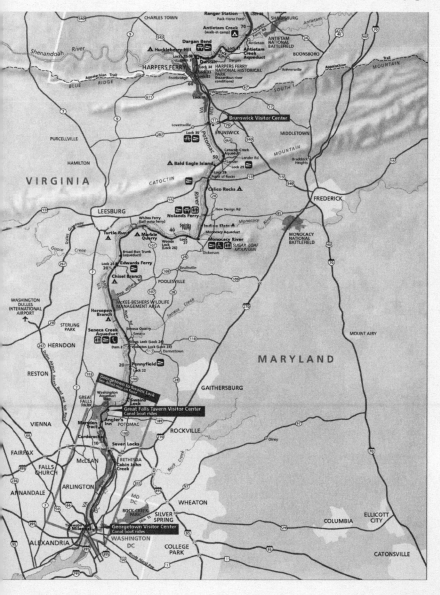

CONTENTS

"Running away will never make you free."

—KENNY LOGGINS

CHAPTER ONE

BIRTHDAY WISHES

It was my birthday, the day I made up my mind to leave. I'd been thinking seriously about escaping for nearly a week, ever since Visiting Day when Mom showed up and I could see nothing had changed at home. Then, that night, someone peed in my one pair of boots. But that birthday cake was the trigger. It set everything in motion. And by then, I had a plan.

Bet you didn't think losers in prison could actually get a birthday cake, did you? But yeah, we did. The last Friday of each month we celebrated—if you can call it that. In the cafeteria, after evening rec and showers, Mrs. Fielder, our sweaty-faced cook, brought in this big chocolate cake in a pan with white frosting, blue gel writing, sprinkles, a couple candles, the works. I was fourteen years old. What's so pathetic is that it was the first birthday cake I'd had in about eight years. Wouldn't have been half bad, I guess, getting a birthday cake for once, even if I did have to share it with the other September birthdays. But the minute I saw what was written on that cake, my stomach clenched up and my breath caught in my throat—Tio's name was on it, too. Just me and Tio.

"Digger and Tio," Mrs. Fielder announced way too cheerfully. It was creepy hearing our two names strung together like that, but Mrs. Fielder didn't have a clue. Looking rather pleased, she set the cake down on the cafeteria table in front of us while most of the boys, slumped back in their plastic chairs, sang a pitiful version of "Happy Birthday." Some of them didn't sing at all, and even those who did, you could tell no one had his heart in it. They just wanted to get it over with so they could eat cake, which we would all agree is far better than half a baloney sandwich on dry bread and rancid fruit juice for our evening snack. Their voices rose with a tad more enthusiasm toward the end—*Digger and Teeeee-ooooooo*—while my head spun like crazy because the bottom line was this: my name was written *above* Tio's on that cake, which meant things would come to a head fast.

"Digger, go ahead and make a wish," Mr. Rankin said. If I had to pick one, Mr. R. was probably my favorite counselor. He set his beefy hands on his hips and, as he caught my eyes, smiled kindly and nodded once. We'd had a talk that afternoon about "if/then thinking"—you know, if you do this, then that might happen—and he was probably hopeful some of it sank in. "Blow out one candle," he instructed. "Then let Tio blow out the other one."

I knew this was a test and I had to make up my mind quickly. I could breathe slow, count backward from ten, try to go with the flow. But I was burning inside because I still wasn't over the humiliation of walking around in those damp, stinky boots a week ago. Ever tried to clean urine out of your shoes with a Kleenex? Let me tell you, it doesn't work very well. Everywhere I went, I stunk up the place. At least I knew who was behind it. My eyes flicked over to Tio and back. Unsmiling, he sat up stiffly, his chin up, his eyes narrowed, and rested his tattooed hands on the table directly across from me. No way was he going to accept seeing my name above his on that cake. That's how small and mean he was. Maybe it was 'cause of his half-a-brain gang mentality. I don't know, and frankly, I don't care.

Still, I swallowed hard. All the other boys were quiet but perked up by then, scraping their chairs back and leaning forward, watching me like hawks. They were waiting to see what I'd do 'cause with my hesitation and all, everyone could feel the tension.

"Go ahead," Mr. Rankin urged gently, and I glanced at him again, hoping that brief look could say what I couldn't: that I didn't hold nothing against my counselors and I hated to disappoint them. Mr. R. and Miss Laurie, the mental health lady, they tried hard to set me straight. It wasn't their fault I couldn't change. I was doing what I had to do, which was get one up on Tio before he got one up on me. And then get the hell out of there and make it home in time to protect my mom and my little brother and sister.

I stood up and, while staring down at the cake, drew in a chest full of stale cafeteria air that still smelled like canned corn from dinner. Quickly, I wished to myself that Tio—and my father—would die miserable deaths; then I leaned forward and blew both of those candles out.

Stone silence.

"Sorry," I said softly, pulling my shoulders back while two tiny wisps of smoke drifted away. I shrugged and looked at Tio. The slightest hint of a smile may have crept on to my lips. "Looks like you don't get no birthday wish."

It worked.

Tio jumped up out of his chair so fast he knocked it over behind him. The little car thief may be short, but he was fast. In a flash, he lunged forward, picked up the cake with both hands, and threw it at me hard. I jumped back on my toes, and to the side quick, like a batter avoiding a fastball, low and inside, as the cake whizzed by. It hit a kid named Jimmy smack in the chest, then slid down the front of him, leaving a huge ski trail of frosting on his sweatshirt. He stood up, spreading out his arms, like *what the heck?* And the pan clattered to the floor.

What a sorry sight. And all that chocolate cake ruined. I felt a pang for Mrs. Fielder 'cause I'm sure she worked hard on that cake, and then stayed after her shift was over to see us get it. All her efforts gone in two seconds. I have to say, I knew exactly how she felt. I once cooked a cherry pie—first and only pie I ever made—for my mom, to surprise her on Valentine's Day. But that night, before we even got to eat any of it, my father came home messed up, picked up that pie, and heaved it across the room. He missed my mother that time, but what a mess—pieces of pie and glass all over the wall, all over the floor, my mother screaming, my brother and sister crying, and me, getting my face pushed into it and my butt kicked at the same time. So no, I didn't have the heart to look at Mrs. Fielder—or time to dwell on wasted efforts—because Tio was springing up onto that table like a wildcat coming after me.

"Tio, stop!" Mr. R. hollered. "Stop right there!" But Tio didn't take orders very well.

I was ready for him. Balled up my fist hard and ducked as soon as Tio's two feet hit the floor and he took a swing at me. Then I popped up fast and smacked him one square on his jaw with the hard ridge of my knuckles. A direct hit, it sent him flying back against the table, then onto the floor where he tried to get up but couldn't and fell backward again. Poor jerk had a short memory. Didn't he remember that I knew how to fight?

He may have been stunned for a second, but Tio wiped the blood from the corner of his mouth, spit, and threw a long, angry look at me. Suddenly, he jumped back on his feet, but Mr. R. and another counselor grabbed his arms to hold him back while Mrs. Fielder yelled into the radio: "Staff support! Kitchen!"

Tio's no weakling. He started yanking and bucking like a frickin' bronco until he tore away from the counselors. Rushing forward, he came after me again. The boys, all of them on their feet, moved aside, giving him a wide, clear path.

"Get him, Tio!" somebody called out.

But I also heard an encouraging, "Go, Digger!" and I'd

wonder later if it was my old friend J.T., 'cause it sounded like his voice. Hard to believe, though, because J.T. and me—we had pretty much stayed away from each other ever since that wrenching ride out to western Maryland in the prison van.

Tio lunged and tried to grab the front of my sweatshirt. But again, I was too quick for him. I came up under his hands with my own strong wrists and knocked them clear away, making him spin around at the same time. Then I kicked him in the can, and he fell forward onto the floor where Mr. Rankin plopped down on him and pinned Tio's arms behind his back. He's a big man, Mr. R. You can bet Tio wasn't going anywhere with Mr. R. on his back. Honest, I had to stop myself from laughing at that point.

Another counselor stood to block me, but I was done fighting for the night. I brushed off my hands and looked kind of longingly at the cake all over Jimmy and the floor. This other boy, Alex, ran his finger through some of the frosting on Jimmy's sweatshirt and licked it. A couple of the boys laughed softly, but the rest hung back without another word. None of them wanted to be caught laughing at Tio, or making wise-cracks, 'cause they knew they'd pay for it down the road.

Weird, but all at once, a quiet kind of sadness settled over the entire room. Guess it was dawning on us all at the same time, the realization that nobody would be eating cake or getting any kind of snack that evening.

Just as I'd hoped, Tio and I were separated for the night. It was a gamble for me, starting that fight, but it paid off because they took Tio to stay in the nurse's office where he could be supervised. I was sure to be punished, too, but like I said, I didn't plan to be around so it didn't bother me. Mostly, I wanted Tio out of the dorm that night so I could finish up what I had to do and get out of there.

Most nights, I'd lie in that hard bed for hours thinking back on the crime that put me and J.T. at Cliffside Youth Detention Center for nine months. We sabotaged a kayak is what we did. Put holes in it so it would sink. It started out as a practical joke, but it went way the heck wrong 'cause a little boy died on account of what we did. What *I* did anyway. Believe me, what I did is a hundred-pound weight I got to carry around the rest of my life. But that didn't mean my mom and my brother and sister had to suffer, too, which is why I was breaking out of that place. So that night, my mind was focused on something other than my crime.

In the morning, the day I escaped, I was all business. I had KP duty, so four of us—me, Haynes, Jake, and TaJuan— we were up at six A.M., half an hour before the others. We dressed quickly, made up our beds for inspection, and then walked over to the dining hall with a counselor. I was relieved to see Mrs. Fielder wasn't the morning cook 'cause I don't know if I could've faced her after what we did to her cake the night before. When we got to the kitchen, we hung up our sweatshirts and made sure our white T-shirts were tucked in. We also had to put on an apron and a KP duty hat, which is just a hairnet like old women wear, but I'm sure they didn't want to call it that or none of us would've worn it.

Haynes and Jake, they got to work cooking up scrambled eggs and bacon, while TaJuan and I laid out the cold stuff: cartons of milk, juice, yogurt, and boxes of cereal for the kids who didn't eat eggs. Everything in prison is cheap. Even the cereal is genetic. Or is it generic? Whatever. The word that means cheap. Like instead of Cocoa Krispies it's Cocoroos, and Fruity Pebbles are Fruity Diamonds. We got a kick out of that sometimes, only that morning I wasn't laughing. Secretly, I pushed a small box of them Cocoroos deep down into the pocket of my pants, because who knew how long it would be before I could eat again?

At seven A.M., the rest of the boys shuffled in, half asleep. Everyone took a tray and got in line. I ate as much as we were allowed and drank an extra carton of milk, then went back behind the counter to start cleanup. While the others left, us guys on KP started washing dishes, sweeping the floors, and putting stuff away.

Here's where it got hairy: at eight A.M., classes started. It was Saturday morning, so we didn't have like English or math. Instead we had this class in drug education and life skills. We were supposed to bring our notebooks with us to breakfast and go straight to the classroom when we finished KP, but what I did was tell Mr. R., who taught the class, that I forgot my notebook and could I please run back and get it? I knew he'd walk me back to the dorm, but I was hoping he wouldn't actually go all the way in there with me—and he didn't.

Alone in the dorm, I moved fast. First, I got the notebook

from the little shelf above where I keep my boots at the end of my bed, then I moved five beds down the line to Tio's. I had wanted to do this the night before, but the stupid guard didn't nod off with his head down on the desk around three A.M., the way he usually does. I turned around to be sure no one else was there and put my notebook on the bed behind me. Then I flipped back the blankets on Tio's bed, yanked down the zipper of my pants, and peed all over his sheets and pillow with everything I had. Quickly, I zipped back up, and redid the covers. Tucked 'em in, too, nice and neat. Ha! Wait'll he got a whiff of that, I thought. Stage Three of our Moral Judgment Development Program said to treat others as you would have them treat you. Otherwise known as the Golden Rule, right? He did it to me, so I guess he wanted me to do it to him.

Quickly, I scooped up my notebook and rushed back outside. Right then, that's when I heard the garbage truck coming in, and my heart started pounding.

"Shoot!" I exclaimed.

"What *now?*" Mr. R. asked. He was pretty annoyed by then.

"Cook asked me to put out the garbage. It won't take me a minute. *Please.* I don't want them to get any madder at me!"

Mr. R. shook his head, but then he said, "All right, go."

I stared at him, kind of paralyzed by the thought of what I was about to do.

"Go!" he hollered, throwing up his hands. "The guys are waiting. Get up to that classroom as soon as you're done." He pointed a finger at my face. "I'll be watching for you."

I knew he was giving me yet another chance and it hurt, it really hurt to do this to Mr. R. But while he walked up the hill toward the classrooms, I marched briskly in the opposite direction toward the dining hall. When I opened the door, I could see some frozen pie shells set out on the counter to thaw and I could hear pots clanging in the back. It was just the cook. The other boys had gone on to class and no one else was around. Peering out the door one more time, I checked to be sure my counselor was still walking away before I kneeled and set my notebook on the floor. Then I stepped back outside and bolted around the corner.

It was my one and only chance and my heart beat double time because I knew that if I went ahead with the plan, there was no turning back and plenty of risk along the way. But I was ready. And the way my life was going, I figured I had nothing to lose, so there was no stopping me.

CHAPTER TWO

OUT WITH THE TRASH

A harsh metal screech tore through the air. I knew the sound well: bad brakes. And those particular brakes belonged to the garbage truck making its way down the steep gravel driveway from the main road to the prison.

From the sounds of it, the truck hadn't made its first pickup behind the gym, so I knew I had at least a couple minutes. But I panicked anyway. In my rush, I tripped over a curb and fell, scraping my hands. Pushing myself back up, I sprinted downhill behind the dining hall to the Dumpster and dropped to my knees, reaching underneath for the shovel I'd hidden there under some leaves. Pulling the shovel out, I quickly knocked the leaves and junk off of it, then tossed it into the Dumpster where it landed on the garbage with a soft knocking sound. Nothing very loud, thank goodness.

I whirled around once to see if anyone was watching, then reached for the handle of that side door of the Dumpster, the one you open to throw in trash. But the door didn't open. I tried it again, both hands tugging with all my might, but it was locked up tight. With no time to lose, I took the only other choice I had, which was to jump and grab onto the edge of the Dumpster. I was lucky the container didn't have a cover. Using all my strength, I hoisted myself up. After I got one leg over the top, it was easy. I simply rolled over the edge and plopped down onto the trash.

The fall inside wasn't bad. The Dumpster was half full, so there were plenty of big, black plastic bags full of junk as well as a bunch of cardboard that made for a soft landing. I saw the shovel and reached over to grab it, then sat there, keeping my fingers crossed that I'd survive getting dumped into the garbage truck. If anything went wrong, I could be compacted to death, no question. My dad drove a front-end loader for a while, so I knew how they operated. A set of arms on the garbage truck would pick up the Dumpster, lift it up over the cab, and dump everything into an opening over the cargo bay of the truck. Next, this big compacting panel with a blade at the bottom would start pushing the trash— squeezing and *compacting* it—toward the back. That's what I needed the shovel for—to jam the compacting blade so I didn't get crushed to death. When the garbage truck got to the landfill, or the dump, or wherever it went, the back would open up and I could slip out and make a run for it. I'd hide out for a while, then try to find that highway that brung me out here and follow it back east. That was my plan anyway.

Two minutes seemed like an eternity. I could hear—and feel—the vibrations of the truck rumbling down the steep gravel driveway.

"Come on, come *on!*" I whispered urgently. "Let's go!" I needed things to click along fast. Pretty soon, Mr. R. would be wondering why I wasn't showing up for class. Couldn't take that long to throw a bag of garbage into the Dumpster, he'd be thinking.

Funny how I could picture so clearly everyone in the class where I should have been at that moment. A sea of blue sweatshirts and blue pants, our boring uniform. Half of them boys would be sprawled over their desks with their heads buried in their arms 'cause class hadn't quite started and no one was wide awake. Me, I was always in a half-awake state on account of the fact that I never really slept, but I never put my head down like that. Someone could take advantage if you had your head down.

So I'd be sitting there in class watching Dontaye doodle. Dontaye, who slept in the bed beside mine in the dorm, also sat beside me in most of my classes, and every day I'd watch him illustrate the sides of his paper. Always the same thing: pointed stars and weird letters that were code for his gang back in Baltimore. Seemed like most of those guys—black, white, Hispanic, all of them—had some kind of gang they were connected to back home. Dontaye talked to me about his gang a couple times, like maybe he even wanted me to join it. Wouldn't that be something? If a white guy showed up with Dontaye? Heck, maybe they wouldn't care. I have to say that deep down, parts of that gang stuff appealed to me. Like the reason Dontaye joined his gang is because he didn't have any family taking care of him, which is kind of like me.

Suddenly, the garbage truck was pulling up to the Dumpster, interrupting my thoughts. The metal arms, which screeched like a giant's fingernail scraping down a big chalkboard, knocked and locked onto the Dumpster, like a monster hug. A jolt sent me forward, then back. Grabbing a bag of trash, I dug myself down deeper as the Dumpster got lifted. I tried to brace myself for what was next, but there was no way to prepare for it because all at once everything got flipped over. Bags of garbage, cardboard, pieces of wood, a broken milk crate—and me. I got knocked around pretty good in the process, lost track of the shovel, and landed facedown with my feet up, squeezed between a bunch of garbage bags like a piece of baloney in a stinking sandwich. And boy, did it stink. If I didn't die from the compactor, I was thinking, I might die from the putrid smell.

Plus it was dark in there. When the cover over the top of the truck slid shut with a bang, I couldn't see a thing. Pitch black. But mostly, I couldn't get over how bad it stunk. It made me want to gag. I struggled to right myself and blindly started rooting around for that shovel. I couldn't find it right off, but what I did run into was a ripped-open bag of garbage, 'cause next thing I knew globs of something slimy and granular spilled out over my hands. I swore and cussed out loud. I knew those guys in the cab couldn't hear over the truck noise, so I cussed even louder a second time.

A different motor started whirring and an ear-piercing, scraping sound began. The compactor was moving! It was pushing all that garbage—and *me*—toward the back. I had to find the shovel fast or I was going to end up like a lousy pancake. Ignoring the crap on my hands, I groped around for the shovel but could not find it. And man, I needed it—*fast*.

I felt the gears shift and grind as the truck made its way back out of the prison yard, up the hill. The whirring of the compactor grew faster and louder as everything got slowly pushed toward the back. I kept digging myself in between bags, trying to find the handle of that shovel, but I wasn't having any luck.

The truck moved on, faster, smoother. I figured we were outside the prison grounds at that point, maybe on the road down the mountain. I wondered where the truck would stop next and whether Mr. R. would put two and two together back in the classroom and guess that I'd gone out with the trash. I could just see him, taking a big sip of coffee out of that thermos cup of his, maybe peeling back the cupcake wrapper on one of those nice muffins his wife made, and then setting it down quick when it suddenly dawned on him. He'd step outside the classroom to make a call down to the office, and instantly all the boys would be on to it. Even Dontaye would stop doodling and crack a smile.

The boys would be guessing how I did it, like did I hide out in the back of someone's pickup the way this kid did a year ago? He hid there at the end of the day and rode all the way to Cumberland to a staffer's house where he slipped out and hijacked a car. Amazing, but he got about a half hour down the interstate before they caught him. Hopefully, they'd be checking all the vehicles in the parking lot first, but Mr. R.

might be insisting on the garbage truck theory. Which meant there could be police cars waiting at the landfill. Or maybe the cops would stop the truck on the highway and poke around, looking for me. Anything could happen.

Like a big bug, I crawled over the bags of garbage and kept searching for that shovel. At the same time I had a flash vision of what would happen to me if I couldn't find it. Maybe it would be justice after all. For what I did to be in prison, maybe I deserved to get squished to death like a dumb insect and buried under a bunch of trash. Maybe I was nothing but trash myself. Heck, my father had been telling me that for years!

But my poor mom. She'd cry her eyes out when she heard how I died. It's true that sometimes I got mad at her for not stopping things. But other times, my throat got tight thinking about her, like how she had driven all those hours in that piece of junk truck just to see me on Visiting Day a week ago. She brought that plastic bag of broken-up chocolate chip cookies from the kids and kept trying to tell me about Hank's new third-grade teacher and the front tooth LeeAnn lost, but all I could see was that cheap makeup caked on her face. It wasn't even the same color as her skin and I knew she was covering up another bruise, which meant it was still going on.

If I got snuffed out, then I wouldn't be there to help her. Or protect Hank and LeeAnn! And that made me think about my father. . . . He'd be laughing his head off when he heard I got crushed to death in a garbage truck. Yup. Laugh his fat, bald head off 'cause he'd get a real kick out of it. *I always said that kid was no good. A knucklehead with no brains.* I could just hear him, slurring his words and slapping the table. It made me mad, thinking of my father getting the last laugh. And that got me fired up all over again. I shook all those distracting thoughts out of my head and scrambled like a cockroach when the lights got turned on looking for that shovel.

Finally, my hand touched metal. Was it the shovel? Yes! I grabbed the handle and started wiggling something fierce so I could get down to the bottom of the truck and jam that thing under the blade. I had to move a couple bags around and wouldn't you know it? Another one broke and a bunch of disgusting stuff spewed out like puke. Rotten oranges, eggshells, coffee grounds, soggy paper towels. I just plowed through it, tossing handfuls of gunk aside, until I felt the floor of the truck under my feet. I pulled the shovel down beside me and managed to get it on the floor where I could push it with my feet.

The truck stopped again, so I did, too. I waited and was quiet, listening. Couldn't hear anything though. Then all of a sudden the top pulled back and sunlight poured in. They were making another pickup, and I had to brace myself for the onslaught of more trash that came pouring down on top of me. I put my hands up to stop stuff from hitting my head. Lucky for me, there wasn't a ton of it that time.

The top slid shut. *Bang!* Darkness again. The truck jerked forward and the compactor whirred. I had to force myself to breathe it smelled so bad, and it seemed like there was less and less oxygen or something. I couldn't get a full breath.

I kept breathing and pushing the shovel with my feet until I heard a loud *ker-chunk* and the whirring stopped. I couldn't move the shovel anymore. Had it jammed the blade?

All I could do then was breathe. Shallow breaths because of the smell. Breathe and wait. Wait and breathe.

A few minutes later, the truck came to another stop. I heard voices and the banging sounds of someone climbing up the side. I had a pretty good idea what was happening. The compactor had jammed all right, just like I wanted it to. But a light in the cab was flashing—orange light if I remembered—so the guys up in the cab would be coming out to take a look.

The top slid open and light seeped through the bags of garbage and trash.

"I don't know!" a guy hollered. "I don't see nothin'. Not from here!"

A long moment passed. No conversation. No movement. If they started rooting through the trash, it was over.

Suddenly, the top slammed shut again and total darkness surrounded me as the whirring, grinding compactor started up again. I closed my eyes tight, hoping the shovel would hold, but almost immediately, I heard a loud *crack!* and felt the handle of that shovel snap in two under my feet.

Everything—including me—was slowly shoved toward the rear of the truck. There wasn't anything I could do to stop it. My whole body got squeezed so hard I couldn't move my legs or my arms, and my face got smashed into a slime-covered garbage bag. Some of that crap actually got in my mouth and made me want to throw up. Then my arm got caught and was pushed up behind my back. I struggled to take more shallow breaths and could feel my face and hands sweat. I never cry—*never*—I stopped cryin' years ago. But I think there were tears in my eyes. I figured this was the end for me.

In that moment, I realized I wasn't ready to die. Maybe I had thought there was nothing to lose, but suddenly I knew how much I wanted to live. I wanted to be with my mom and LeeAnn and Hank again. I wanted to see my grandfather before he died. I wanted a chance for a good life—like maybe I could go back to school and graduate and make something of myself. I once dreamed of joining the Marines.

All these thoughts kind of flashed through my mind. Then, like somebody blew a fuse, everything stopped. No light. No sound. No putrid smell. No vibrations under my feet. Nothing . . . 'cause I must've blacked out.

CHAPTER THREE

RUNNING

Did you ever wake up in the morning and not know what day it was? That's what it was like for me, except I had a lot more to figure out than just the day. I didn't know *where* I was, or, at first, even *who* I was! All I knew is that it was dark, I was running out of oxygen, it smelled bad, and something smooshed against my face. Did I fall down a black hole to Hell? Was I buried alive? What?

Slowly, it dawned on me. Then, like the faucet suddenly got turned on, my whole life gushed out. I was Michael Griswald, only everyone called me Digger. I had a mom, and a little brother and sister back home who I loved a lot. I also had a father who drank and got mean. We lived in the country in a small yellow house with a toilet that didn't work and a lot of junk in the front yard—old tires and parts of the trucks that my father drove. I was thirteen—no, fourteen—years old and I was in prison because I played a practical joke on the rich neighbor who bought my grampa's farm. My grampa is in a nursing home now, but it used to be, when things were bad at home, I could escape to Grampa's. That's why I hated Mr. DiAngelo so much. He was the snooty guy who bought Grampa's farm, tore the house down, then built a mansion there so he could show off how much money he had. One day, he even kicked me and my friends off his property. So I played a joke on the a-hole, only the joke went sour and his little boy died. . . .

For a minute there, the memories stopped. It was like hitting a wall. Everything stopped for me when I thought back on what I done. Which is why I tried not to think back on it. What good did it do? I couldn't undo the past.

I went to prison for my crime, but now I needed to get home, so I escaped in a garbage truck, which is how I came to be squashed beneath a ton of garbage.

The sound of a distant siren pierced the air. I knew if I didn't crawl out of that garbage and disappear, I'd be right back where I came from with even more time ahead of me. I made a huge push with everything I had and created a tiny space with enough room to wiggle my toes—that was good. Next, I moved my feet up and down, then I started clawing at those slimy bags with my bare hands and slowly inched my way upward. I was like a lowlife worm crawling out of that garbage.

Pushing, wriggling, clawing, and kicking, I kept at it until my head popped through into the air and sunlight hit my face. I groaned from the force of one more all-out effort and, breathless, tumbled out and down a huge slide chute of slick garbage bags. When I landed at the bottom of that trash mountain, I took a minute to suck in big gulps of air, so much that I thought I'd crack my ribs. It wasn't exactly fresh air, but let me tell you, it was better than anything at the bottom of that pile.

The siren sound grew louder. Definitely time to get going. The sun was bright and directly overhead, so I figured it must've been around noon. Surely they were on to me now 'cause I had split just after breakfast.

Looking around, I didn't see anyone else at the landfill. Dense woods surrounded the place, but I spotted a gravel road that led in and out. The best thing, I decided, was stick to the woods, but parallel the road so I didn't get totally lost. My legs were cramped up from being crushed by all that garbage, but I hobbled away and as soon as I got the kinks worked out of my muscles, I started running. My boots weren't exactly great for cross-country, but I ignored the heaviness and ran like a jackrabbit until I was deep in the forest.

I stopped once to take off my sweatshirt 'cause I was sweating buckets. Tied the sweatshirt around my waist and kept going. I jumped over logs, plunged full force through briars, sprinted uphill, and sidestepped quickly down a rocky hillside like a mountain goat. I could feel a stone in my left boot, but I didn't stop to get it out. I trotted on through a patch of pine trees where the needles made a soft carpet, slogged through a muddy swamp that tried to suck my boots right off, then jogged through a high-grass meadow until I came upon a shallow stream.

The water looked clean, so I lay down on the ground and

took a long cold drink. While I had my face in the water it dawned on me that the police might try to track me on land and that I might do better by walking up the stream. It was right then—before I plunged my foot in the stream—that I heard the helicopter overhead.

Thumpathumpathumpathumpathump.

That would be the state police looking for me!

Glancing around, I spotted a bunch of juniper bushes nearby, then dashed up the hillside and threw myself beneath the prickly branches.

I knew a little bit about those helicopters 'cause my old friend Brady had a cousin Carl, who was a paramedic. Carl took us with him one day to the state police barracks in Centreville to see a state chopper that was parked there. It was a twin engine Dauphine Europcopter and we actually got to sit inside. This guy, this pilot who actually flew choppers in Vietnam, explained all the controls and showed us that special camera underneath the helicopter nose. It was called FLIR, which stands for Forward Looking Infrared. I never forgot that because that camera was so cool. What it did, it could tell temperature differences on the ground and things would show up black and white on this little screen in the cockpit. Like a human body? It's warm, right? So the camera would pick up that a warm body was on the ground and flash an image to the pilot. Even if it was dark out, the camera could do this.

I dug myself in best I could, hoping that camera couldn't get a picture of me if I was curled up in a tight little ball beneath the thick bushes. That or else they'd figure I was an animal or something.

Lying there, making myself as small as possible by hugging my arms and legs, I listened as the chopper noise grew louder and louder, finally passing directly overhead. I lay still, barely breathing, until the helicopter's sound grew fainter, like a distant heartbeat in the sky.

I didn't want to take the chance of getting spotted, so I decided to hide out for a while. Hidden by the bushes, I sat up and took off one boot to shake a stone out. Then I took off the other boot, too, and peeled off both socks so they could dry out a little. Everything was wet and muddy from sloshing through that swamp. I saw big blisters on my feet, but there wasn't anything I could do for them so after a while I put my damp socks back on in case I had to leave in a hurry.

About that time, I realized how hungry I was and felt for the box of Cocoroos in my pocket. But I decided I'd better save them for when I was *really* starving. In my other pocket, I found a balled-up Kleenex and my white card.

I took the card out and was getting ready to flick it into the water down below, but then I realized that the card could float downstream and become a clue. I held it in my hand and looked at it. They give us that card the first day we signed in at Cliffside. It was about four inches by four inches and laminated so we could keep it in our pocket all the time. We were told to memorize it, all the tiny print, front and back. Like we had to recite the twelve problem areas us boys fall into and the four most common thinking errors we make, plus a whole lot of other stuff so we could change our ways.

I knew the whole thing. Memorized it the first week just for something to do. With my eyes closed, I could repeat the entire card, starting top left with those twelve problem areas: low self-image, easily angered, inconsiderate to others, aggravates others, authority problem, alcohol or drug problem, stealing, lying, etc.

Yup. I must have gone over that list a dozen times with Miss Laurie, my mental health counselor. I liked Miss Laurie. She was pretty, with long dark hair she pulled back into a ponytail. She wore pink fingernail polish and interesting earrings, always something dangly. And she smelled good, too. First two days I was in her office I didn't say a thing, and she didn't care. She said it was okay to just sit there if I wanted. She offered me candy from her jar and I took a piece, a little Hershey bar. I sat there eating chocolate and watching the angelfish swim around in their tank for a full hour.

"Anything we talk about in here stays here," Miss Laurie told me. "I don't report back to juvenile detention."

But still I didn't talk. She did paperwork while I watched the fish and picked at a hangnail.

Along about the third or fourth time, Miss Laurie played a game of cards with me and talked about her little boy, Harrison, and how he painted himself with Magic Markers. I couldn't help it. Her story reminded me of my little brother,

Hank, and how he drew pictures all over himself with an ink pen so he'd look like my tattooed uncle Chip. I cracked up remembering that. Guess that's when I started talking to her some. Mostly about Hank and LeeAnn at first, then my mom and finally, my dad. We also talked about the twelve problem areas.

My response was always the same. I told Miss Laurie I was only guilty of three of those areas. Easily angered, no question. And I did occasionally aggravate others, but only after they aggravated me. And yes, I told her, I was guilty of misleading others. No question how I led my friend J.T. down the wrong path, which landed both of us in prison. I told J.T. I was sorry and that it wasn't his fault. I told the judge that, too, in court. I spoke up and said J.T. didn't do nothing, that I did everything myself. But the judge, she wasn't even looking at me when I said all that. She was busy writing in her folders. When she was done, she took off her glasses and stared at me. She said J.T. stood guard, which helped me commit the crime, so he was guilty, too.

There wasn't anything I could say or do to change her mind. Me and J.T., we were put in this white prison van, just the two of us in the back separated from the driver by a big wire grate. We had these heavy shackles on our feet, and handcuffs on, too. But neither one of us was gonna try to escape or anything. We were like stunned that day we were convicted and rode quiet all the way out to western Maryland in that van.

It took nearly four hours to get to Cliffside. There wasn't

any music or anything to listen to. The driver had his radio on low, but it was just talk radio, religious stuff, and we couldn't really hear it anyway except for an occasional "praise the Lord" or "the Bible tells us . . ." Wasn't a whole lot to look at neither. You couldn't look straight through that grate between us and the driver or you'd go cross-eyed, so all we could do was look out the side windows. I hadn't ever been all the way out to western Maryland before and I would have to say, the countryside was nice, especially the hills. There weren't many hills I knew of on the Eastern Shore.

A couple hours into the trip, the van climbed up this mountainside so steep my ears popped. Then we passed through this big slice in the top where huge cliffs rose up above on either side of us.

"Ain't it something?" the driver called back to us while he drove between those multicolored cliffs. He turned his radio down. "It's called Sideling Hill."

Neither one of us answered, but I did look out the window.

"See that black layer toward the bottom?"

Again, we didn't say anything, but the driver continued: "I heard that black layer has got marine fossils in it, which means this here area was underwater—a huge sea at one time. Yup. From eastern Ohio all the way to western Maryland. Imagine that!"

I did try to imagine that. Why not? I didn't have anything else to do. I wondered how come the sea disappeared, and how the floor of it ended up on top of a mountain! I looked at all the multicolored layers in those cliffs and wondered what stories each one had. Kind of wished the driver would say some more, but once we were through that pass and headed down the other side, he went back to chewing his tobacco and turned up his radio.

I kept glancing at J.T., who was sitting across from me, but he never once looked up. Not even at the cliffs on Sideling Hill. He just stared at the floor the whole time, which was incredibly depressing. I had really ruined his life.

At one point, a big tractor-trailer full of logs roared past us, and I remember thinking I was just like one of those cut-down trees strapped onto the back of that truck, with no power over my life anymore. Then we came across some guys in bright green neon vests who were picking up trash in the median strip, and I saw a van parked alongside the road that had the words INMATE LABOR on it. I wondered if that was my future. Would that be me one day? Picking up trash by the road while other people drove by and stared? I dropped my head. I sure didn't want that for a future.

Suddenly, there wasn't time to be thinking of my life or that sad trip out to western Maryland because the sound of barking dogs brought me back to the present right quick. Instead of tossing that white card in the bushes, I slipped it back in my pocket and reached for my boots.

CHAPTER FOUR

HOT-WIRED

Plunging my feet, boots and all, into the nearby stream I started running—hopping rocks, splashing between boulders, sometimes sinking in up to my knees. For hours I thrashed through that water. I figured it was my only chance to lose those tracking dogs.

Finally, I took a break to catch my breath. It was getting dark and I didn't hear the dogs anymore, just the sound of that stream moving around me and the pounding of my own heart in my ears. I was really whipped so I climbed up out of the water onto the bank. A fallen tree in a hemlock grove overlooking the stream caught my eye. I walked up the hill and practically collapsed under some of the branches. I decided it was a good place to stay overnight since I could be hidden and yet I could still see things coming my way. In the distance, I caught a glimpse of some traffic moving on a busy road and hoped it was that highway that brung me out to western Maryland.

After I rested up, I gathered a few loose boughs and wove

them in and out between the branches of the fallen tree to make my shelter against the wind thicker. I also threw a few boughs underneath so I'd be a little bit off the ground and hopefully not get so cold.

When my so-called bed was ready, I unwrapped the sweat-shirt from around my waist and pulled it on. It was a bit cool, just right if you ask me, but I knew it would get colder over-night. Out here in the mountains, even on the warmest days, it got downright cold at night. I sat down to take off my boots and, boy, what a stink. My socks weren't just wet and dirty, but bloody, too, on account of the blisters had popped. There wasn't time to dry anything, so I shook the socks out and put 'em back on.

My stomach was rumbling and I probably should've held off on the only food I had, but I got weak and gave in. I pulled the Cocoroos out of my pocket, tore open the box, and wolfed down the cereal in three handfuls before think-ing anymore about it. Which was another one of my prob-lems. *Stop and think first,* Mr. R. liked to say. *If I do this, then that will happen.* The ole if/then thinking. But that cereal was gone. Oh, well. Too late. I shrugged and stuffed the flattened cereal box back in my pocket so I didn't leave a trail. See? At least I wasn't completely stupid.

Boy, I felt like an animal curling up under those evergreen branches to sleep. And yeah, I guess I was a little scared. Not much, mind you, but a little. Noises in the night woke me a couple times. I worried 'cause I didn't have a weapon or anything. If a bear came along, I wasn't sure what I'd do. Plus it wasn't very comfortable. I turned on my side, but my arm didn't make a very soft pillow. And I got cold, especially my feet, which were still wet.

When the first soft light of dawn seeped through those hemlock boughs, I was ready to move again, even if I was starving hungry, sore all over from sleeping on those branches, and a little stiff from the cold and dampness in my feet. I rubbed my arms to get warm and trudged on through the woods, keeping that road in sight the whole time. When I saw a bunch of cars and trucks parked, I crept up closer and hid behind some bushes to get a better look. I saw gas pumps and a building and wondered if I'd stumbled across a rest area, or a restaurant of some kind. It was a nasty thought, but I wondered if there might be some garbage to look over.

When I inched up even closer, and could see down to the far side of the parking lot, I realized it was a truck stop because a whole row of big tractor-trailer rigs was lined up side by side. My brain started buzzin' then because I knew how to drive those trucks—even better than I could drive any car. We had a big rig parked behind my house for years when I was growing up. My dad hauled a lot of baled hay in it, down to Northern Virginia, up around Baltimore to fancy horse farms. He hauled watermelons and corn in the summer. And every once in a while he hooked up a "reefer"—one of those refrigerated trailers—down to the processing plant in Salisbury and took a bunch of frozen chicken up to Boston.

I went with my dad on a lot of those trips so I could help him unload. I was only eight, nine, ten years old at the time.

It was a lot of work for a little kid, but I never minded a lot of work. I thought it was fun spending the night in the sleeper and chowin' down diner food—meat loaf and mashed potatoes, big pieces of lemon meringue pie, and something called chicken-fried steak. All of that food was better than anything we had at home 'cause my mother didn't like to cook much on account of her headaches.

Meeting other truckers was fun, too. They were pretty nice to me. I met a guy from Oklahoma once at a truck stop. He sat on the front bumper of his rig, leaned over, and whittled a piece of wood with his jackknife. His hands went fast, while the wood shavings fell and made a tiny mound on the ground between his feet. When he finished, he handed me a little hand-carved buffalo that's still on my bureau at home.

Mostly, I just liked being out there on the road with my dad. He wasn't real bad back then. I mean, he slapped me around some, sure. Seems like I could never do right by him. And he drank, too, but then he'd sleep it off before we drove long stretches, and those long stretches were downright pleasant. My dad was like a regular person then. We even told jokes and sang along with the radio. I remember thinking this is the way dads were: one day they're pissed off and slapping their kids around, the next day they're buying them root-beer floats and letting them skip school.

About the time I turned ten my dad taught me how to drive the truck. I was lucky I was tall for my age, 'cause I never would have been able to reach the brakes or push that clutch in. My dad said if he ever got "incapacitated" (which I took to mean drunk) I'd have to be the one to get us home. So I listened up and learned early. And I have to say, it was a ton of fun. I loved driving that big rig.

Squatting by the edge of the parking lot, I plucked a piece of grass and chewed the end of it. No doubt in my mind, I thought, if I could get inside one of those trucks, I could take it miles down the road and really put some distance between me and Cliffside.

I threw the grass away and tried to look kind of casual as I walked behind the building and over to the row of trucks. I sat down at a picnic table and—*unbelievable*—a big old Kenworth came rumbling in and stopped smack in front of me. I knew it was a Kenworth just from the way it looked: the shape of the hood, the windshield, the smokestacks, the location of the lights. But that grille bonnet proved it. Because there it was, big and silver: the Kenworth emblem, which looks like a shield with bars runnin' up and down and a circle in the middle with a big KW, the K over the W.

Vocabulary is not my thing, but I tried to think of the word: *predestined*? *preordained*? Well, anyway, pre-*something*! My dad's rig was a Kenworth and I knew that truck inside and out. I turned my head away and dropped my jaw as in, *do you believe this*? But I stayed quiet until the trucker climbed down out of the cab. Hiking up his jeans and putting a cell phone to his ear, he started walking toward the restaurant. He limped on one leg, and over the crunch of gravel I heard him say, "I'm stoppin' to get somethin' to eat. This little place here off sixty-eight, they make great biscuits and sausage gravy . . ."

So he wasn't going in just to use the restroom or get a cup of coffee. He was going to sit down and eat great biscuits and gravy. Man, I would've liked to put away some of that breakfast, too. Just thinking about it made me drool, but this was my big chance and I didn't have a lot of time to waste.

As soon as that guy disappeared into the building, I walked up to his truck and looked it over. Of course no trucker would leave his keys in the ignition. But starting the truck wasn't the problem. So long as the truck was a diesel built before 1992—and it looked like it was—I knew I could hot-wire the thing from underneath. See, the old diesels were combustion engines, not electric like the new ones. You couldn't hot-wire a new truck like you could this one. Getting inside the truck was the challenge for me.

Okay. I saw right away that just behind the driver's door was the outside entrance to his sleeping compartment, and that underneath was a smaller door, which was his toolbox. (My dad used to stash a bottle of vodka in his toolbox.) I took a look around but didn't see a soul, so I opened the toolbox door and reached my arm way up inside and felt around. Sure enough, there was a lever that popped open the door above to the cab's sleeper. Only reason I knew about that lever was 'cause my dad was always losing his keys or leaving them inside the cab and this was how he broke into his own truck. For a second, I sort of spun halfway around and smiled. I couldn't believe how easy that was.

When the door popped open, I moved quickly, stepping up and throwing myself inside, right on the guy's bed. It was

real comfy and had a soft brown blanket and a couple pil-
lows. I was thinking I'd take that blanket with me when I left.
Between the sleeper and the cab there was a little closet and
I could see the trucker had two shirts hanging in there, along
with a thick gray jacket. I'd take some of them clothes, too, I
thought. Maybe, if I had time to rummage around, I'd find
some dry socks.

No time to lose though.

I crawled through the sleeper into the cab and lowered
myself down in the driver's seat. So far, so good, I thought, as
I started throwing things around, trying to find the right tool
to start the truck. On the console between the two front seats
I found a jackknife and pushed that in my pocket. Found a
Snickers bar, too—my favorite!—and tore into it right away,
taking a huge bite. Next, I came across three folded dollars
and change and stuffed that in my other pocket. All at once,
I remembered the toolbox. I'd check that for what I needed,
I thought, but suddenly what I needed was right smack in
front of me on the console: a screwdriver.

After grabbing that screwdriver, I reached down to the left
of the steering wheel, to pull a T-handle into the override
position, which basically opened the fuel valve under the
truck. And one more thing: I unlocked the driver's-side door.

Screwdriver in one hand, I shoved the rest of that candy
bar into my mouth and slid out, partially closing the door so
I could get back in fast. I cast another glance around, to be
sure no one was watching me, then I bent over and crawled
behind the huge front tires, beneath the truck.

I had barely enough light to see under there, but I knew what I was doing. I went directly to the starter location, just under the cab, and found the two wires I needed: the large positive cable that runs to the truck battery, and the smaller wire that hooked up to the ignition system. Using the screwdriver, I crossed those two wires, hoping they would spark and fire up the engine. I tried, but no luck. Nothing. Disappointed, I finished chewing, then swallowed the chunk of candy in my mouth and tried again. This time, it worked like a champ and that old Kenworth *roared* to life. Made my heart jump it was so loud!

Still hunched over, I backed out with the screwdriver in my hand and climbed up into the driver's seat in the cab. The truck's engine was vibrating like crazy and blowing black smoke into the air through the silver smokestacks on either side of the cab. The truck was making a beep noise, too, because the air pressure was low and you needed to build up some pressure in order to release the brakes. The brakes all run by air on those big rigs.

Nervous, I tossed the screwdriver onto the console and sat in the seat, trying to calm my nerves by getting comfortable. I moved the seat up a little, adjusted the mirrors, and kept checking, too, to see if that trucker was coming back. When the beeping stopped, I pushed in the two circular disks on the front dash that released—to a huge burst of sound— the two parking brakes, one for the trailer and one for the tractor. I bit my lip so hard it bled a little—I could taste it— then carefully pushed down the clutch with my left foot and threw the stick shift into reverse. With my hands clenched on the steering wheel, I glanced in the rearview mirror to be sure I had room—those trucks take a lot of room when they turn—but everything looked clear, with plenty of space. So I pressed my right foot down on the accelerator and backed that big baby out of the narrow parking place like a damned pro.

Even though it was a ten-speed truck—not a fifteen or an eighteen like the newer ones—I knew I'd go through several gears pretty fast. First gear, then second, third, fourth, and fifth. The truck was rumbling something fierce, still blowing smoke and groaning with each gear change, but that's what they did, those trucks. They made a ton of noise, but you got used to it pretty quick.

I wasn't but a couple hundred yards down the exit ramp when I needed to throw the splitter so I could get the truck into sixth gear. I simply reached down to a button on the gearshift and with two fingers pulled it up. Instantly, the gears shifted and I was in sixth with no problem. By the time I pulled out onto the highway, I was launched into seventh gear with a great big smile on my face.

CHAPTER FIVE

MILE MARKER 72

Out on the highway, I got that truck rolling. In hardly no time I was in ninth gear and cruising along at fifty-five miles an hour. Seemed a little fast, though, so I eased up and downshifted once, but mostly for practice. Boy, I was really in trouble now, I thought. Breaking out of prison and then stealing a truck. I smiled when I thought about it, yeah, but it wasn't 'cause I was evil or anything. I hadn't *hurt* anyone so I figured I might as well enjoy the ride.

On the console, I noticed two things I'd passed over earlier: a pack of gum and a red Southern States cap. I didn't want anyone to look in my window and realize it was a kid driving, so I slapped the cap on my head right away. Then I took a piece of gum, unwrapped it with one hand, and pushed it into my mouth.

Weren't too many cars on the road so I took my time and kept glancing at the dashboard to familiarize myself with it again. It was a dizzying array of dials and gauges. Some I could remember what they were, like the air pressure gauges.

They were important 'cause, like I said, those brakes run on air and you needed to know what kind of pressure you had. I also knew about the rpm, the revolutions per minute, that the motor was making. The faster you went, the higher the rpm. You had to keep an eye on that 'cause you could burn things up if the rpm got too high.

I checked out the fuel gauge, too, to see how much gas I had. One tank was full, the other about half. Each tank carried about 120 gallons. When gas gets as high as four dollars a gallon, it must cost pretty near a thousand dollars just to fill up the rig. No question I had plenty of gas to get me a good distance, but I was thinking I'd go just until I got to a city, or a small town, where I could park the truck and take off again. By then, the state police and everybody else would surely be on to all this.

In fact, why didn't I check that out? Reaching up over the rearview mirror, I flipped on the CB radio and turned to Channel 19, the truckers' channel. As a kid, riding with my dad, I loved listening to those guys chatter back and forth.

First thing I heard on Channel 19 made me tense up: "Hey, there, westbound, there's a smokey ahead of you with radar . . ." A smokey—that's a cop—and he had speed radar out. I didn't know if that message was for me or not. Quite frankly, I didn't know if I was headed east or west, which was pretty important. But I didn't have a clue about the lay of the land out there in western Maryland, and even if there was a frickin' GPS in the cab, I wouldn't have known how to use it. But just in case it *was* me headed toward that smokey, I eased up on the accelerator so I wasn't exceeding the speed limit, which I guessed was fifty-five or sixty miles an hour.

For a long time I chewed that gum hard and focused on driving that big rig. I finally saw a big sign that said I was headed east, toward Frederick and Baltimore. *Yes!* I hissed to myself. That's the direction I wanted: east. I have to say, I was really enjoying that ride. I even thought that if I didn't become a Marine, that maybe one day I'd be a trucker instead 'cause I liked driving and I could be my own boss. You have to be sixteen to get a Class B license to drive a truck, but that was only two years away for me. I even started wondering what I was hauling in that trailer behind me, and whether it might be some kind of food, and if there was any way I could get inside to take a look.

I was going up and down some big hills and seeing lots of pretty, open countryside with fields and stuff. I come to a town once, but I was going too fast and blew right by the exit ramp so I just kept driving. I had to downshift some to slow her down and take some mean twists and turns through that town. Almost sideswiped a guy in a station wagon and nearly rammed into a bus that was going too slow. But all in all, I did pretty good. And let me tell you, driving that truck through traffic was better a hundred times over than any video game I ever played in my life.

Once I got outside of town on the open highway, I opened up and put some miles on that odometer. More big hills, then a mountain—Polish Mountain it was called. I wondered if that was some kind of a joke, only the sign for it looked legit.

I dropped down to sixth gear and kept to the right lane, pulling twenty to twenty-five miles per hour up the entire incline. I cruised down the other side in the same gear, but with the brakes on, too. Easy, I thought. I could do just about anything with this truck. The problem would be police after me as soon as that trucker got done eating his biscuits.

When I spotted a police car traveling west, I got nervous and pushed my foot down on the accelerator. Then another mountain come up. Again, I pulled into the far right lane to go slower, and kept checking the rearview mirror.

Something about the mountain seemed familiar and when I got to the top—the Kenworth was really groaning by then—I realized it was Sideling Hill with the big cliffs and the colorful rock layers. I remembered that prison van driver talking about the marine fossils and I couldn't help but turn my head to take a look. Sure enough, I could see that black stripe in the rock, and it made me wonder all over again how in the world this mountaintop could have been under the ocean. Seemed so upside down, I thought. Just like my life! I still held this against my mother: the fact that when I was only eight, nine years old, I was taking care of my brother almost all the time. Then, when my baby sister was born, I took care of 'em both, like I was their dad or something. I mean, I was fixing meals and changing diapers and putting those kids to bed—everything. And I was just a kid myself! The only times I got a break from it was when I was in school, or working with my dad, or when I snuck out to be with my friends.

Boy, I realized then that I should not have let my mind wander like that because I was already starting down the other side of Sideling Hill way too fast. I slammed on the brakes and hoped I didn't jackknife, but nothing happened. The truck kept picking up more and more speed.

Then I smelled burning rubber. My brakes were heatin' up. If the brakes got *too* hot they'd fry themselves—even catch fire!

I glanced at the temperature gauge for the rear axle and could see it was already over 200, which meant trouble with a capital *T*. I sat up straight, my heart thumping high in my chest and the palms of my hands sweating. I checked out the rpm to see if I could downshift to slow the truck, but I was already closing in on 2000. Think about this: a truck just idling is 800 rpm; out on the highway it's around 1600. So when you get up to 2000 rpm or more you are going way too fast to downshift. You're redline! In other words, your ass is in the danger zone. BIG TIME!

Faster and faster I went. My hands were gripped on the steering wheel so tight I didn't think I'd ever get 'em pried off. Both my feet were pressed down on the brake and I was praying, too—which for me was just pressing my lips together and hardly breathing—'cause by then I could smell smoke. And where there's smoke there's fire, right? My brakes were definitely burning!

My heart beat triple time but I was blanked out on what to do. I remembered my dad saying that in an emergency he'd run the truck off the road and up an incline and let it fall over. But the only incline I saw was the one I was flying down. Both sides of the road simply dropped off.

So how would I stop? Would the truck launch into the air like a rocket and crash? Should I take it over the side so I didn't kill nobody else? What?!

I tried pumping the brakes, lifting both my feet and slamming them back down, but that didn't do squat. What else could I do? My eyes stretched wide as I stared at the road and the end of my life coming up fast and furious on the black pavement in front of me. In the opposite lane up ahead, two cars were slowly climbing the hill. Would they call someone? The police? Or 911? Could they tell I was in trouble? Did they even *notice* me?!

Probably not. To every driver I passed, I was probably just another annoying trucker, the guy they hated getting stuck behind. I was a blip out of the corner of their eyes, a big truck rumbling down Sideling Hill on Highway 68. Why should they take notice? Why bother if you're cruising along in your spiffy, big SUV, listening to music or chatting it up on your cell phone?

And you know what? That reminded me of something. Not that I dwelled on it 'cause my life was like hanging in the balance at that time. But I had this flash feeling that I'd been there before. Later, I realized why that not-being-noticed, invisible feeling seemed familiar. It's because I have been in a million everyday places in my life—like the Food Lion or Wawa, or the gas station with Mom, or even at school shooting the breeze with my friends—and I must've seemed like a perfectly normal kid. A kid buying milk, pumping gas, laughing at a joke—when all the time what people saw was a shell, the outside of a kid who was totally different inside 'cause he was holding stuff back to cover up the fact that he lived with a grizzly bear at home.

Even my best friends didn't know about my other life. I did my best to hide it, which is why they hardly ever came over to my house. True, I was embarrassed that we didn't have a flush toilet that worked, that we had to use an outhouse. But more important, I didn't want them to see my mom and dad screaming at each other, or me, getting my arm yanked out of my shoulder or my head pushed into the wall. I don't know when I figured it out, but it finally dawned on me one day how it wasn't normal for parents to beat on their kids the way my dad did to me. And I didn't want my friends to find out about it 'cause I was afraid it would scare them off, and I didn't want to lose them.

The word *RUNAWAY* flashed by.

I can't tell you how many times I wanted to run away from home. Only I didn't 'cause of LeeAnn and Hank. Mom, too. And Grampa! I was always afraid my father would get mad at Grampa for helping us, and that he'd hurt him, too.

RUNAWAY TRUCK.

Hey! Did anyone care that I was about to die?

RUNAWAY TRUCK RAMP.

Okay! Okay! Yes! The sign said a runaway truck ramp was coming up. One quarter of a mile. Un-frickin'-believable! That was exactly what I needed! A gift from heaven if there ever was one!

I came around a bend at seventy, eighty—maybe a hundred miles an hour, I don't know, I didn't want to look—and the rpm had hit 2100. The smell of burning rubber was everywhere and I knew fire was eating up the brakes—maybe even the rear axle! If oil leaked out of the oil seal near the brakes, it would fuel the fire even more.

At mile marker 72—some things you never forget—the runaway truck ramp come into view. I gritted my teeth and turned the steering wheel slightly to the right. Let me tell you, the truck shot down that ramp like a bat out of hell. At the far end, I could see how the ramp went uphill. I held tight to the steering wheel and the truck stayed smack in the middle of the ramp, following the decline of the mountain. But soon, like maybe three hundred feet, the entire rig sank into the thick bed of pea gravel like a bowling ball rolled into a hole full of cotton. Amazing, but that tractor-trailer truck came to a complete stop in just a few seconds. Then, with a shudder and a quick jolt forward, it stalled out.

I blew the air out of my cheeks and sat there, my eyes fixed straight ahead and my hands still glued to the steering wheel. But not for long. When I got my wits back I sucked in my breath and got out of there fast. I didn't even turn around to see how much of the truck was on fire. I simply reached back into the sleeper to grab the blanket and yank the trucker's gray jacket off a hook, then I kicked open the door, spit out my gum, and took off.

CHAPTER SIX

THE WRONG WAY

Blanket under one arm, jacket under the other, I sprinted downhill and across a field. I whipped off the trucker's red hat so it didn't draw attention and just kept running. Only once did I shoot a quick glance back. I didn't see anyone or anything except for that big old truck sunk down in pea gravel with smoke curling out of its rear end.

After thirty, forty minutes I was out of breath and slowed to a walk as I rounded a cow pasture. A couple of black-and-white Holsteins stopped grazing to look at me. But I picked up the pace again and kept jogging down this long hill toward the woods. When I came out the other side of those trees, I saw an amazing scene that stopped me: a wide river cut through the countryside with a little stream running parallel to it. A well-worn path ran in between. What the heck?

No one was around so I walked over a little bridge that crossed the smaller stream and came to stand on the path. I was confused by it. I mean I could tell from the hard-packed dirt and gravel that the path got a lot of use. And not only walked on, but, as I soon found out, *biked* on, too. I had to duck into some bushes quick when a couple people on bikes came along. I stayed hidden after that, and walked close to the path, but not *on* it. Occasionally, more bikers came and each time I ducked into the bushes, or kneeled down behind a rock. I moved this way the entire afternoon until evening closed in. That's when I stumbled on another interesting sight: a long tunnel that carried the path through a hill.

At dusk, when I didn't think any more bikers would be riding by, I entered that tunnel. It was dark as the ace of spades in there I couldn't even see my hand in front of my face—so it's a good thing they had a wooden railing 'cause I sure didn't want to fall into the murky stream that run by the path. I kept one hand on the railing, the other arm in front of me. Surrounded by darkness, every little crunch my footsteps made echoed. I could hear water dripping off the old brick walls, and it was so cool and damp I got goose bumps. Creepy. But I saw enough bikers go into that tunnel that I knew it had to empty out somewhere.

When I finally came out the other side it felt good to have some light, even if it was the dim light of dusk. I spotted a couple picnic tables and outdoor grills, plus a map covered in plastic and nailed up on a board. The map said I was at a campground in Paw Paw (how's that for a name?), West Virginia. *West Virginia?* I was going the wrong way for sure! Although this also meant the police might not be hunting for me there.

I found out the name Paw Paw came from some kind of local fruit. Then I learned that I had just walked through the Paw Paw Tunnel, which was part of the C&O Canal towpath on the Potomac River. Huh. *Canal towpath.* I had no idea. None! An old black-and-white picture showed some mules pulling a barge along the canal. Guess this is how they moved cargo and stuff before there were railroads and trucks.

I studied the map and could see that the towpath went all the way from Cumberland, Maryland, in the west, to Washington, D.C., in the east. I was disappointed I'd lost so much ground going the wrong way. But if I turned around, I could now follow the towpath all the way to D.C., then find my way east, to the Eastern Shore of Maryland.

Suddenly, I heard noise—the sound of breaking sticks and voices. Then I smelled smoke. Not burning rubber this time, but a good smoky smell, like a campfire. Quickly, I crouched and pushed my way under some bushes near a big tree. I pulled the brown blanket up over my head and shoulders and while I sat there, smelling that campfire and waiting for night to come on, I realized how hungry, thirsty, and tired I was. But mostly hungry.

It was Sunday, so back at Cliffside they probably would have eaten already. Dinner was early—5:15 every day. A lot of the boys complained about the food, but I didn't think it was half bad. I remember our first meal exactly: a cheesesteak sub with potato wedges, catsup, carrot sticks, and banana cream pie. I thought it was pretty darn good for prison food, especially compared to what I might have had at home, which most likely would have been a peanut butter sandwich, if there was any bread, or a bowl of cereal. Sometimes, me and the kids, all we had for dinner was them little Goldfish crackers.

I couldn't get the thought of that cheesesteak sub out of my head. I had practically inhaled it I was so hungry. While I ate, I had looked around at all the other boys in that dining hall the first night, all of them hunched over and busy eating. It wasn't anything like my middle school cafeteria where the noise would've been deafening. Nobody was talking at Cliffside. No chitchat or food fights or laughing. Nothing. Just forks and spoons—no knives, mind you—scraping away at those hard plastic dinner trays. And I remember thinking this: none of those boys looked like criminals to me. They looked like they could have been boys back at my middle school! Or down to the high school where I should have been a freshman. . . .

After we ate, us new kids had orientation in the prison office. First thing a nurse took our temperature. I guess to make sure we weren't sick and bringing in some awful disease. Then we got our hair shaved off and were told to get undressed. We had to put on the Cliffside uniform, which was a white T-shirt, blue pants they called Dickies, and a blue sweatshirt with the name of Cliffside Youth Center on it. Guess they didn't want to advertise the "detention" part of the name. Everything we wore that day, like my jeans, my shirt, even the L.L. Bean watch that my grampa gave me when I turned twelve, all that stuff got put into a bag and sent home. It was like prison stripped away who you were.

Then we had a lecture about how we'd have to do chores and go to school, stuff like that. Get this: we would get a dollar a week and two stamps. And we'd be allowed to make two twenty-minute phone calls.

It was really humiliating. All of it. But don't forget, I had just ridden out to that place in a prison van with handcuffs and shackles on my feet. I was already beaten down from being in court. I was accepting things as they came because I was guilty. I had done wrong, and I was willing to pay for it. So I went with the program. I wasn't scheming to get out or anything. Not then. Even with Tio and a couple of them others, I probably could've done the time. But then Mom came to visit, and, like I said, I needed to get home to protect her and somehow fix things.

After we put our uniforms on, they piled up our arms with a load of supplies: sheets, pillowcase, two blankets, socks, boxers, another T-shirt, another pair of blue Dickies, light blue pajamas, a black field jacket, gloves, a wool hat, and boots. But before we left for the dormitory we had to put everything down and fill out a bunch of paperwork about our education and sign promises to obey the school rules. It was pretty basic stuff like: "When the teacher is talking, be quiet and listen . . . Raise your hand to be recognized . . . No writing in your textbooks . . . Always do your best work." We had to promise not to send emails, or download any pornography or gun material from the school computers.

A lot of rules. Later, when we got a tour of the place, I saw a sign in the rec center—and don't get the wrong idea that this rec center was some incredible entertainment place. It wasn't even like a big room or anything, just the basement of a cabin that had a pool table, a TV, and some video games. It all seemed pretty low-key, but when you walked in, a big sign said: NO FEET ON WALLS. Which made me think it got kind of rowdy in there sometimes.

Finally, we had to sign a pledge acknowledging that "everyone has the right to be treated with respect." Which brings me to my good friend, Tio.

Tio arrived same time as J.T. and me, but in the other van which had brung kids from Baltimore and some place called Montgomery County. First thing you notice about Tio is that his head is like too big for his body, which is short, but really muscular. I think he must have worked out with weights and stuff. Second thing you notice about Tio is his thick, dark curly hair. Let me tell you, there was a mass of it before they shaved it off, which left his head looking like a shiny melon. A real melonhead.

Next thing you see is either the cold look Tio had in his eyes, or else all his tattoos. He was covered with 'em—his hands, his arms, the back of his neck, even his face had a little design on it, up near his ear, and a single-digit number was tattooed at the corner of his eye. I couldn't help but stare at Tio 'cause he was the most weird-looking person I had ever seen.

"So what's crackin'?" he asked, fixing his eyes on me hard, like I had a hell of a nerve to breathe and be in the same room with him.

Of course, I didn't know what the heck he was talking about, but already I didn't like his attitude and I was *not*— I repeat *not*—gonna be pushed around by any punk kid at that place.

"What's *crackin'*?" I repeated his question and stared back at him. "Maybe your head will be *crackin'* in a minute."

Boy, that got him fired up. He lunged forward and tried to take a punch at me right then, right there in the office during orientation! Mr. R. had to step in quick and put Tio in a headlock. "You just signed your name to a paper there where you acknowledged this is a *hands-off* program!" he hollered. "Do you have any idea what that means?"

Tio didn't reply. He looked like a big June bug wriggling around and trying to swing his arms, but Mr. R. had him locked up tight.

"Everyone here has a right to be treated with respect!" Mr. R. yelled.

Tio strained to look up, but Mr. R. had him facing down. Still, I could tell that Tio had zero respect for me. So I made it mutual. And that was the beginning.

Wow. I must have fallen asleep there in the bushes. It wasn't very restful sleep though 'cause I was leaning against a tree and the rough bark made ridges on the side of my face. When I woke up everything was pretty quiet, except for a couple frogs croaking away. You could also hear the slight murmur of the nearby river. The campfire was out. The only thing I smelled was the vague garbage odor from my own clothes.

I heard an owl hoot and I kind of smiled 'cause I liked the sound. Reminded me of listening to owls when I slept on the back porch at Grampa's farm, or camped out with my friends, J.T. and Brady. Could have been that owl woke me up. Bet he was hungry, too. A gentle breeze rustled the bushes. I rubbed at the sore ridges on my face, but the first thing I really thought about was food.

They say you don't make good decisions when you're tired or hungry. Well, I was both. But I had to at least check out those campers, didn't I? See what they had?

CHAPTER SEVEN

HARDEN THE HEART

Slowly, I baby-stepped through the shadows, trying not to crunch any leaves or make any noise. Lucky for me, there was a good bit of moonlight. Between the tree branches, I could see it reflect off the water, making a sparkly silver path across the Potomac River. When I got close to the campsite I kneeled down. I was close enough to see a few glowing embers from a dying fire and make out the silhouettes of two different tents. To my right, not far away, several bicycles leaned against the trees, almost all of them with saddlebags over the rear wheels.

I crept over to the bikes and ran my hands over one. I didn't feel a lock or a chain on it. Guess these campers thought they were safe out in the woods. I explored all the saddlebags looking for food, but no luck. I went back to the bike on the outside of the pile and could tell from the fat, knobby tires and the tread that it was a mountain bike. I knew a kid back at school had a mountain bike with twenty-four gears that cost like over a thousand dollars. He let me ride it once, over a cornfield, down a gully, and into the woods. It was awesome.

In the dark, the mountain bike's metal handlebars were cool and smooth beneath my fingers. The bike had the twist shifter instead of the trigger kind. You twisted back for easier gears, forward for the harder ones.

Quietly, I picked that bike up and moved it a few feet to the trail.

Looking back at the camp, I suddenly noticed that overhead, hanging by a rope in a tree, were several backpacks. That would be their food, I guessed, strung up to keep it away from critters. With my eyes, I followed the line of rope to where it was anchored to a nearby tree. Piece of cake, I thought, untying the knot at the base of the tree and slowly letting the rope out. When the backpacks were on the ground I fumbled with the knot on the rope, but it was too complicated so I pulled out the knife I stole from the trucker, opened the big blade, and sawed through it.

After pausing to listen again, I folded and slid the knife back in my pocket. I picked up one backpack and was about to explore what it had inside when I stepped on a big stick that snapped in half with a loud *crack!*

Immediately, I heard a voice from one tent—then two voices—then a click—then light spilled out of one of the other tents!

Quickly, I put the backpack on, dashed for the bike, and hopped on.

"Hey!" someone called after me. "Stop!"

I slammed my feet on the pedals and pedaled like a madman, twisting the shifter forward to put the bike into a harder gear so I could cover more ground. But the gears went crazy and the pedals spun around with no traction at all!

"Come back, you thief!" one of the campers called out.

Finally, the gears caught. I practically jumped on the pedals to get the bike going and pumped hard. Zipping into the black tunnel, I had to imagine the path when it disappeared. Imagining wasn't good enough 'cause right away I smashed into the brick wall dripping with water and got scraped off the bike. I hit my head hard and sat on the ground, stunned.

Forcing myself up, I grabbed the bike's handlebars and started running while pushing the bike beside me. I kept it between me and the wooden railing, hoping the railing would stop me from falling into that murky canal.

A little glimmer of light up ahead gave me something to aim toward. I hopped back on the bike and pedaled furiously again, flying out the other end of that tunnel like a guy whose pants were on fire.

With only moonlight it's a miracle I stayed on that towpath as long as I did. I leaned forward and kept pedaling. I covered a lot of ground this way, too—maybe as much as a mile—before the accident.

I don't know what I hit, but all at once I was off the towpath, in the air, and crashing hard against the ground. When I got my bearings I realized the backpack was gone and that in another inch I would have been over the edge into that stew pot of a canal.

In a panic, I patted the ground all around me, found the backpack, and threw it back on. I lifted the bike by the handlebars, but when I hopped on it, it wouldn't go and I could tell the front tire was punctured. That bike wasn't going anywhere anymore. With both hands, I picked up the bike and heaved it deep into the brush. Then I took off running into the woods.

I paused once to listen and when I heard voices and saw a tiny headlight approaching, I threw myself flat on the ground.

Seconds seem like minutes when you got your face pressed into a bunch of dirt and wet plants that had who-knew-what kind of insects crawling all over them. But—this is a weird thing to say—I also kind of liked it. I bet the Marines did stuff like this all the time. It was a challenge, but it was saving me and I knew I could live through it—that I could *endure* it.

Boy, and I knew that word *endure*. It was on a sixth-grade spelling test once. *Endure* means to "harden the heart . . . to hold out, to last." I remember when my teacher read the definition for that word out loud, how I dropped my head and slid down in my chair. Even my face got hot 'cause that teacher could have been talking about me! That word *endure* applied to like my whole life. I had hardened my heart all right. I stopped crying in about the fifth grade. And some nights, the whole night, when I was a kid, I slept in my own backyard at home so my dad couldn't find me during one of his rages. When we still had the big truck, I'd curl up in the sleeper. But he found me there once and whupped me good.

So I got me this other spot behind the toolshed where I had made a shelter with sheet metal, old tires, and a broken-down lounge chair. So no. I never forgot that word *endure*. I *lived* that word.

I kept taking shallow breaths and listening. Soon, two bikers cruised by on the towpath with their little bouncing lights. They didn't see their bike in the bushes. More important, they didn't see me.

When I figured they were far down the path, I stood up. But instead of returning to the towpath, I walked through the woods to the edge of the river. It was rough walking. In some places, there was no beach at all, just rocks. Big, small, round, sharp—all kinds of rocks. I ended up in the water half the time, but I waded quietly, close to shore and kind of hunched over so I couldn't be seen. One time, I had to climb over a bunch of boulders and one of my boots slipped. I went down hard. The backpack broke my fall, but then I slid sideways, cutting and tearing my pants at the knee.

I walked this way all night until a few birds started singing and faint traces of dawn turned the sky purple. Then, out of nowhere, I stumbled on this boat ramp. A sign said: LITTLE ORLEANS DRIVE-IN CAMPING. And next to the ramp were two overturned canoes.

Staying low, I snuck over to the canoes. It would be a change of pace to paddle in a canoe instead of walking. Fun, too. I chose the dark green one and not the silver one 'cause I thought silver would draw more attention. But when I went to lift the end of the canoe, I discovered it was chained to a stake in the ground. Both canoes were chained up.

Disappointed, I sat on the grass and crossed my arms. But then I had an idea. I tried moving one of the stakes back and forth, back and forth, until I felt it start to get loose. I worked at it until the stake gave way and I could pull it out of the ground. Quietly, I lay the stake and chain in the green canoe, set the backpack on top of them, and started pulling the canoe across the grass.

At the water's edge, I took off my boots and socks, and gently placed them in the bow. Then I rolled up the bottoms of my pants, although I'm not sure why 'cause they were already wet.

Stepping into the cold water I felt the pull of the current. I was several feet out in the river beside the canoe when I remembered the paddles. Damn! I cast a glance backward and scanned the area, but I didn't see any. What I did see was a police car slowly coming down the dirt road. Like a snake, I thought, sneaking out of the bushes to get me.

Quickly, I ducked down and pushed the canoe out to deeper water. When I felt the water halfway up my shins, I pointed the canoe downriver and rolled over the gunwale the way a high jumper rolls over the bar. Flat on the bottom of the canoe, I curled up and stayed low while the boat drifted with the current. The whole time I expected someone to call out to me from shore, but the only thing I ever heard was water rippling down the sides of the canoe.

After a while I sat up and discovered I was a good ways

down the river with the landing out of sight beyond a bend.
Another close call. Unbelievable.

Guess some people thought the river was a floating trash
can 'cause I saw a ton of disgusting stuff out there in the
water: tires, a little kid's wading pool, a car seat cushion, tin
cans, bottles, a Styrofoam cooler, dirty diapers, a broom.
When I saw the broom, I reached out and grabbed it. Even if
I couldn't paddle with it very well, at least I'd have something
to push the canoe off the rocks if it got stuck.

I lay the broom down inside the canoe and sat for a while,
watching the sun come up in the east over the trees. It was a
right pretty sunrise and I wondered what the day was going
to bring. But my stomach was making a lot of noise again so
food was my next order of business. Here's what I found in
the backpack:

Two bottles of water

A tiny red flashlight that worked

Small box of waterproof matches

The C&O Canal Companion, a guidebook sealed in a Ziploc
bag

One asthma inhaler, which I held in my hand a full minute
before I figured out what it was

Food! Two apricot Clif bars, a package of organic beef
jerky, buttermilk pancake mix, a Baggie full of raisins, and
one package of dehydrated oriental-style spicy chicken.

Right off, I drank an entire bottle of water without stopping, I was so thirsty. Then I chowed down one of the Clif
bars, swallowed a handful of raisins, and bit into one of the

beef jerky sticks before stopping to save some of that food for later.

I felt better, but I was still pretty tired from all the running. I folded up my sweatshirt and put it on the bottom of the canoe for a pillow, pulled the trucker's red hat from the jacket pocket to lay over my face, then stretched out to rest.

Now, I know what a person might be thinking at this point. Like did it bother me I broke out of prison? That I stole a tractor-trailer truck and burned up its brakes? Did I feel bad for ripping off that trucker's jacket and his knife and his hat and his three bucks? Was I crushed with guilt because I took someone's backpack full of food? Then stole and gave their bike a flat tire? Did I ever stop to consider it wasn't very nice to uproot a chained canoe and take it down the river?

The answer is no. The answer is *hell, no.* I did not ever stop to think about whether what I was doing was right or wrong and what the consequences might be—the if/then thinking stuff. Later on I did, sure. I knew what I did was wrong, but I didn't feel awful about it 'cause I had my reasons. No way did I have that *conduct disorder* thing that Miss Laurie talked about. She said if I beat up kids and didn't feel guilty about it that it could be a warning sign. She tried to scare me, I know she did, by saying if I had that disorder I'd probably spend most of my life in prison and end up getting killed before I was twenty-five years old. But, like I said, I knew I didn't have that disorder. I never beat up a kid who didn't deserve it. And let me point out that I did feel bad when I saw that asthma inhaler thing in the backpack 'cause I knew this girl in middle school who needed to suck on hers all the time or else she couldn't breathe.

Yeah, and let me say something else, too. When you are on the run you don't stop to think about right versus wrong, or what will happen if you do *this* or *that*. You sure as heck don't worry if you have conduct disorder. No way! 'Cause if you have hardened your heart like me and you're on the run, you don't pussyfoot around! You block everything out and keep moving in a forward direction. Straight on, man, because your life is on the line.

I don't know how else to say it. *You keep moving to survive.*

CHAPTER EIGHT

PALINDROME

A big *clunk* startled me. I sat up fast and swiped the hat off my face. The canoe was wedged between two big rocks. I grabbed the broom and started to push off, but there was this strange whooshing noise behind me. When I turned around I saw I was about a hundred yards away from going over a dam.

Whoa! That would not be fun. I dropped the broom and figured I'd better get out of that canoe fast! Quickly, I took the jackknife and the cash out of my pockets and stashed it all in the little front pocket of the backpack so it wouldn't get wet, then I rolled over the gunwale into the water. I gasped it was so cold! Deep, too. I couldn't touch bottom, which made me nervous.

I got hold of the rope attached to the front of the canoe and wrapped the line around my hand twice so I could pull the canoe free. On my back, one hand holding the rope, I kicked as hard as I could. But BAM! The canoe smashed into another rock.

I realized then that there were so many boulders in the

river I could hop from rock to rock pulling the canoe instead of trying to kill myself by swimming. So that's what I did.

On shore, I dragged the canoe to a small clearing and pushed it under some bushes. Then I sank to the ground, untied the soggy jacket from around my waist, and wondered: what next? Keep moving? Hide out for a while? I couldn't decide. First things first. I really needed to pee so I got up and did that. Then, hungrier than ever, I carried the backpack over to a moss-covered ledge hidden by some brush and sat by the river. I was soaked from head to toe, which was downright uncomfortable, so—after taking a good look around—I stripped off all my clothes, except for my underwear, and set everything on one of the rocks to dry. It felt weird, being out there practically buck naked, but I was also glad to get those stinking clothes washed off 'cause every time I got a whiff of garbage it made me kind of sick to my stomach.

Rummaging through the backpack, I decided on two more pieces of beef jerky and five raisins, all of which I laid out beside me on the rock.

While I ate, I thought I'd check the C&O Canal book to see if I could find out where I was. A map inside showed the Potomac River and a line of dashes and dots that were the towpath. Both sides of the river had railroad tracks, too. I found the Little Orleans campsite where I stole the canoe and ran my finger down the river to a bar labeled Dam No. 6. That's where I was, I figured. Above Dam No. 6.

Maybe, I thought, I could pull the canoe around the dam and continue paddling downriver. At some point, I'd start walking the towpath again, but I kind of liked that canoe. Along the way, I'd have to find more food. Some towns were coming up. I still had three dollars in my pocket. But I could also do some Dumpster diving. It wasn't much of a plan, but it's all I could think of just then. That reminded me of the Joker in the movie *The Dark Knight,* saying, "Do I look like a man with a *plan?*" Funny. I loved that movie.

So there I was: a kid with a plan, beside a canal, and out of the blue, this pops into my head: *A man, a plan, a canal: Panama.* I smiled, recalling how that was a palindrome. It's the same thing, forward and backward. Like the name *Hannah,* or the words *racecar, nun,* and *toot.*

Ha! Me and my friends used to have fun with oxymorons: *jumbo shrimp, pretty ugly, plastic silverware.* But if you ask me, we had even more fun with palindromes. *Madam, I'm Adam.*

Still grinning, I turned my face up toward the sun.

Don't nod.

I chuckled. There was a kid at my middle school named *Mike Kim.* His whole name was a palindrome!

Boy, my mind sure wandered, didn't it? It was right about then that I heard whimpering in the bushes. Little, high-pitched whimpering sounds. Startled, I swung my head around to see who was there, but all I saw was a squirrel frozen halfway down a tree. Standing up, I scanned the river-bank. Nothing toward the dam. But a small motion upstream caught my eye. Like a little furry hand, waving.

Barefoot and with just my underwear on, I carefully picked my way over a few rocks to get a better look. It was a dog. A little gray dog lying on its side. It was stuck somehow and its tail was flapping up and down.

"Hey, buddy," I said calmly. "You okay?"

When he heard me, the little dog whined and his tail started thumping like crazy. I crept closer and saw a clothesline had been wrapped around its neck and that the line was tied to a small tree that was caught up in the rocks. The dog was drenched to the bone, his tongue was hanging out, and his head could barely move on account of the rope was so tight.

Kneeling down, I touched him softly on the side. "It's okay," I told him. I wondered what kind of lowlife would tie a rope that tight around a dog's neck.

"I'll be right back," I promised.

I returned with the knife so I could free him. There was no collar or anything on the dog. Maybe he'd run away from a bad situation—like me. When I finished cutting him free, he tried to stand up but couldn't, and I had to help him. When he finally got his four legs square under him, he shook himself off and licked his chops. I thought he was gonna bark, but he started gagging instead. He coughed up some water, then hobbled toward the river to take a drink.

The dog was really skinny, like you could see his ribs under his gray fur. When he finished his drink, he gazed up at me with water still dripping from his mouth. He had a cute face with dark eyes and ears that sort of flopped over.

"Don't get any ideas," I warned him. "I don't want no dog trailing after me. I don't have any extra food."

But the dog didn't trot off.

"Go on. Go home!" I ordered, pointing upriver. I even kicked dirt at him.

Still, the dog didn't budge.

Great, I thought, rolling my eyes. What did I get myself into this time?

I returned to my backpack and sat down to eat the two snacks I had laid out.

Of course you know what happened, right? Exactly. The dog followed me and sat in front of my face looking so starved and hungry that I gave in. I gave him a nice piece of the beef jerky, which he didn't even chew, just swallowed whole. That did it. I was *not* gonna waste food on a dog that didn't even taste his food.

I tried to ignore the dog. I finished the jerky that I laid out, and the raisins, too, one at a time. But the dog just sat, watching me. When I laid down with my hands behind my head to take a rest, the dog stretched out, head on his paws, beside me.

My mind is always jumping around and I started thinking about random things again. Like how I didn't want a dog, and even kicked dirt at it, but how I also fed it and so now it was lying down beside me. I was like a palindrome myself, I thought. Forward and backward all the time. There was no direction in my life. I wondered if that's what religion did for people, straightened them out so they'd know what direction to go in all the time. Plenty of times I wished I had religion like J.T., who read the Bible and went to church regular, including at Cliffside where a minister from a nearby church preached in the dining hall Sunday mornings.

Even Abdul, the boy who slept in the bed beside mine back in the dorm—and the first Muslim person I ever knew—made me envious sometimes 'cause he seemed so calm, and had a real purpose in his life, which was praying five times a day. First thing Abdul did when we come back from dinner was get out his black rug and go out into the room where we lined up our laundry baskets. It was the only place he could go for privacy. They stopped letting him wear his hat, his kufi cap, because the other boys gave the counselors grief about it, like why couldn't they wear a hat, too? But Abdul was cool about it. He told me it didn't matter to Allah whether he was wearing his kufi cap. What mattered was what was in his heart. . . . Although I did wonder what Allah thought about all the shoplifting Abdul done to get himself into Cliffside.

I don't know. I wished I had religion sometimes 'cause I wanted to believe there was someone or something big enough to reach a hand in and fix things up. But it hadn't happened in my life yet. So I could never decide what to think about God. It's like I wanted to believe in *something*, but I didn't know what.

I opened my eyes then and saw a huge "V" of geese honking their way across the sky. The birds were so high up they looked like tiny dark spots in a big ocean of blue. It was late September—were they coming or going? The sun was so bright I had to close my eyes.

Do geese see God?

I smiled.

Another palindrome.

CHAPTER NINE

A REAL FRIEND

"*T*hink of the other person," Mr. R. was telling us one night as we sat around the campfire. "Before you lash out or say something nasty, think of how your actions will affect that other person." He never gave up on us. I had to admire Mr. R. for that. "TOP thinking," he called it. "Think of the Other Person."

He would have been proud then, 'cause I was indeed thinking of the other person. I stared through the flames at my old friend J.T. As usual, his head was down, but when he glanced up I caught his eye. Was he coming with me or what?

I couldn't tell. So in the darkness, I rushed to get a place in line right behind him. "What's your answer?" I asked softly, close to his ear.

"Stupid!" he hissed as we headed back to the dorm.

I didn't know if he meant that I was stupid, or the idea was stupid.

He turned his head slightly. "Why do you have to go and run anyway?"

"I told you why. I gotta protect my mom and the kids."

"How are you going to do that? Your dad's bigger than you are."

"Not by much. If I have to, I'll use my baseball bat for protection."

"What?" J.T. turned all the way around and stopped the line. "That bat I gave you for your birthday?"

"If you were a real friend, you'd come with me," I said quickly.

"Yeah?" he spat back. "If you were a real friend I wouldn't be here in the first place!"

Did he pull back his hand to hit me?

"Yo! What's going on back there?" Mr. R. hollered.

I threw up an arm to protect my face—a dog barked—I woke up!

My eyes flew open. It was a dream. Only a dream. J.T. didn't know I was going to run. And of course he wouldn't have gone with me—I wouldn't have asked! But his words echoed in my head: If you were a real friend I wouldn't be here in the first place!

The dog barked again. I rolled over and followed his gaze. Some bikers were stopped on the towpath across the river. Had they seen us?

"Shhhhhh!" I scooped up the dog in my arms and held his muzzle shut. "You want to get me turned in?"

I sat there in my underwear, holding the dog, and looked down at my clothes, still drying, on a rock close to the river. Boy, was that dumb, I thought.

When the bikers left, I let go of the dog and scrambled down to get everything. The pants were still damp, but I put them back on anyway and, staying low, returned to the canoe to fetch the backpack. It was late afternoon by then and I was hungry again. I knew I should have rationed out the food but I didn't have the willpower. I ate the second Clif bar, then drank the second bottle of water, figuring I could refill it with river water if I had to.

At dusk, I pulled the canoe out from under the bushes and dragged it through a tangle of thickets and over rocks until I was past the dam. The water made a ton of noise pouring over that dam. It was only like a five-foot drop, but it would have swamped me for sure.

I walked to the edge of the river and refilled the empty plastic bottle, hoping the water wasn't full of pollution or tiny bugs or something. Then I closed my eyes and chugged the entire thing. It didn't taste bad, so I refilled the bottle for later.

Lucky for me, there was still some moonlight left. When it was time to go, I pulled the sweatshirt on, but kept the jacket tied around my waist. I stuffed my socks into my boots and tied them to the backpack. Then I rolled up my pants and waded into the river alongside the canoe.

Behind me, the dog whined softly. I'd hoped to get away quick 'cause I felt bad about leaving him. But with all that whining, I gave in and went back to shore briefly to scratch his head. "Sorry, bud," I told him. "I can't take you. You gotta go survive on your own now, okay?"

The dog held up his paw, like for me to shake it.

"It was good to know you, too, bud. You'll be all right."

Then I turned, quickly pushed the canoe farther out, and hopped in. I didn't look back until I was a good ways out. The dog was just sitting there, a dark spot on the moonlit shore, like he was waiting for me to return again. I felt a twinge in that hard ole heart of mine. But what was I going to do with a dog?

I faced forward and kept paddling.

Even with the moonlight, it was hard to see things on the river and occasionally I'd hit a rock or ram into a log. A broom doesn't make a great paddle. I used up a whole lot of energy making very little progress and got plumb wore out doing it. The bristles in the broom started falling out, too. The more I paddled, the less broom I had. I took off the sweatshirt— I was so hot—and sat for a while with the broom across my lap letting the canoe drift with the current. Sometimes, the current would spin me around and I'd go backward.

One time, while I was drifting, my eye caught something running along the shore. A fox maybe? A deer? I kept my gaze fixed on it and shook my head when I realized it was the dog.

Crazy mutt, I thought. He didn't give up easily.

Next thing I knew, the dog was barking his head off. I squinted, but couldn't quite see him anymore and wondered if he'd run into a raccoon or a skunk—or a possum maybe. Possums had sharp teeth and could be pretty nasty. I thought of going in to shore to help him, but then I heard a funny, vaguely familiar sound. The canoe was kind of sideways so I turned to look forward. Unreal—but another dam was coming up fast! I couldn't believe it was happening *again!* No time to haul butt over to the side of the river—I was going *over* this one!

In the two seconds I had I reached forward to grab the backpack and clung to it like it was my lifeline. Then together— me, the canoe, the backpack, the broom, everything—we went sailing over that dam.

The canoe swung around at the brink and then plunged into the river below straight down, like an osprey diving for fish. The water hit me hard and took away my breath. I struggled in that dark, cold water, kicking my feet and thrashing like crazy until I broke through to the surface.

Gasping for breath, still holding on to the backpack, I tried to swim off so I didn't get sucked under again. Beside me, the canoe popped to the surface, bottom side up, like a dead fish. I reached for it, but the hull was too slippery. With nothing to grab on to, I had to give up and watched it float away, moving fast down the river. In the dark, I soon lost sight of it.

My instinct was to swim toward shore, but I already knew how strong that current was so I didn't fight it. I simply went with it. Holding on to the backpack made it more difficult, but I wasn't ready to let go. I could have untied the jacket from around my waist to lighten me up, too, but I felt like I needed to keep moving my arm to keep me afloat. In the end, I just let myself be carried downstream like one of those old tires I saw earlier. Boy, I could have used one of those tires right then!

Cold, and drifting with the current, I felt myself grow weaker. Every once in a while I'd try to rest my arm, the other arm holding the backpack, and just float on my back, but I would have to admit that I was getting worried.

Suddenly, this animal came toward me in the water. I didn't know if it was a beaver or a giant otter or what. And then I realized it was the dog. The dog was swimming toward me!

"Hey," I murmured. When he got close, I grabbed him, but

ended up pushing him under the water. I let go right away and he popped up, shaking his head and sputtering water. I didn't try again 'cause I knew I was too heavy for him.

"Go on," I said. "Go back."

Right away, the dog turned to swim away. Guess he realized what a mistake he'd made. But as he paddled off, I kind of reached out and lightly took hold of his tail. It must've taken all the strength that little guy had to pull a human being like me through all those currents to the shallow side of the river. But he did it and it was a miracle. A bona fide miracle as far as I could tell.

As soon as my feet started hitting rocks I let go of the dog's tail and crawled the rest of the way out of the river. The rocky bottom hurt my hands and knees, but it also felt good to have something solid beneath me. Breathing hard, heart pounding, dripping wet, shivering, I was a mess. I collapsed on shore with my face pressed against the sand and one of my arms still hooked through one of the backpack straps.

The dog came over to lick my face, but I was too wiped out to thank him. When I did finally push myself up, I saw the dog was curled up right beside me. He saved my life, he did. So he was my friend now. A *real* friend. Right then, I did three things: I gave that dog a good, long two-handed head scratch. I named him Buddy. And I reached into that soggy backpack and gave him the rest of the organic beef jerky.

CHAPTER TEN

THE ANTELOPE
AND THE ALLIGATOR

It was best, I decided, for me and Buddy to walk the tow-path at night because the police had to be looking for me by then. After hiding out all day in the bushes I had pretty much dried off, but my pants were torn in the knee and the jacket, which had been tied around my waist, dried all wrinkly so I was sure I looked pretty beat up.

Walking, all I could think about was food. I knew that there was still a pancake mix and the oriental-style spicy chicken dinner in the backpack. But they were my absolute fallbacks.

The moonlight wasn't as bright as the night before, but there was still enough for me to see things along the way. Like all of a sudden I'm on this bridge crossing high above a creek and underneath I see this beautiful triple-arch thing. When we stopped for a rest, I pulled the flashlight and the guidebook out of the backpack and read that this arch thing was the Conococheague Aqueduct. Get this: it was a *bridge for the canal.* A canal which was dug into the dirt and filled with tons of water once crossed over the creek on this aqueduct. If you were a fish back then that looked up one day, you'd see a boat floating up there. *Amazing!*

Back in 1920, a canal boat busted through one side of the aqueduct and fell into the creek below. The captain's son, walking with the mules pulling that boat, was fast thinking enough to cut the towline so the mules didn't get hauled overboard, too. Those canal boat owners got attached to those mules. I know 'cause I remembered this song, which started going through my head: *I got a mule and her name is Sal. Fifteen miles on the Erie Canal. She's a good worker and a good old pal. Fifteen miles on the Erie Canal* . . .

While I walked, Buddy trotted right by my side, like he was *my* good ole pal. If I stopped, he stopped. If I started jogging, he trotted. We even went to the bathroom in the woods at the same time. Walking along toward morning when we could see better, we saw some pretty sights, like this great blue heron that flew low—like a glider—right down over the middle of the canal. Since the canal isn't used anymore, parts of it have dried up. Huge trees grow in some places and in one grassy spot, a whole herd of deer was grazing . . . *Fifteen miles on the Erie Canal* . . . Once, we saw ten turtles, looked like sliders, clumped together on a log, soaking up sun.

Sometimes, we'd hear these far-off rumbles that turned out to be freight trains going by on the opposite side of the river. I tried to count the boxcars once. Got up to around seventy-five and gave up.

Just about the time I figured we ought to find a place to hide out for the day, we come to this visitors center. I didn't want to get seen, but I was so hungry I snuck around, poking in the trash barrels.

"You're up early," a voice behind me said.

I whipped around and must've looked startled—not to mention embarrassed.

"I didn't mean to scare you," this guy said. He looked like someone my parents' age, only he wore a ranger outfit and had a long, gray ponytail and a big mustache. "I was just opening up for the day."

"Oh . . . yeah, good morning," I replied, trying to sound normal while I sized up the guy and wondered if he might be on the lookout for a Cliffside runaway.

"You hiking the towpath?" the guy asked.

Just then, Buddy caught up and sat beside me.

"Yeah," I said. "Me and my dog, we're hiking the path for a couple days."

"Where you from?" he asked.

I had to think quick. Where was I from? I recalled one end of the trail. "Cumberland," I told him.

"Ah! You're doin' the whole towpath then? All the way to Georgetown?"

"Yup!" I nodded. "All the way."

The guy kind of looked me over. What did he see? The tear in my pants? The wrinkled jacket? The dirt on my face? A little bit of stubble on my chin?

"Well, you might want to keep an eye out for the weather today—clouds moving in. Supposed to be a storm blowing through tonight."

"Thanks," I said. "Thanks very much. I'll keep an eye out."

"If you need any supplies, we sell a few things inside. Bread, peanut butter, water, that kind of thing."

Man, I would have loved some of that peanut butter! But I suspected it cost more than the three dollars I had in my pocket.

"I'm all set." I started walking away fast then 'cause that guy must've wondered why I was poking in the trash and where all my gear was. I stepped up my pace and wondered where Buddy went. Had I lost him already?

All of a sudden the guy shouted, "Hey! Come back here!"

I didn't even turn around, I just took off running. I bet I ran half a mile before I glanced backward. That's when I saw Buddy trotting after me with a loaf of bread in his mouth.

"You little thief!" I knelt down, breathless, and reached out my hand. "Give!" Buddy dropped the entire loaf in my hands. "You're something else, you know it?" I rubbed him on the head.

We went another couple miles before we hid in the woods and dove into that bread. It was plain old white bread, but it was delicious. We ate three pieces each and I washed mine down with sips of river water. I stuffed the rest of the loaf in the backpack, and we settled in to hide for the day.

Buddy went right to sleep, but I couldn't so I pulled out the guidebook again and read up on the dam that nearly killed me, Dam No. 5. It was one of a bunch of dams built on the river to force water into the canal. What's so historic about the dam is that during the Civil War, Stonewall Jackson tried to blow it up. In December of 1861 Confederate soldiers slid into the water at night and started hacking away at the dam with sledgehammers. But in the morning, Union soldiers blasted them with a cannon. There was a big battle over the next couple days, but the Confederates finally gave up.

Wow. Made me feel weird having gone over a dam that was the site of a Civil War battle.

By evening, when I started walking again, I noticed it was clouding up and I remembered the ranger's warning about rain. When it started to sprinkle I headed for cover in this old stone building that had a couple walls and part of the roof missing. It was dark already so I took out the flashlight and shined it on a sign that called the building a lock house. There were pictures of the lockkeeper who once lived there with his family. It was his job, I read, to fill or drain the locks, which raised or lowered the canal boats from one level to another. Cool, I thought, how somebody invented all that stuff.

Inside the lock house, I sat on the dirt floor and took the backpack off. I looked for my sweatshirt, forgetting that I had lost it when we took that dive over the dam. The temperature had really dropped, so I put the gray jacket back on and zipped it up. Buddy lay down beside me. I was so hungry my stomach rumbled.

After sitting there in the dark for a long time, listening to the rain pouring down outside, I gave in and pulled out the bread. I also ripped open the bag of oriental-style spicy chicken. It was all dry and powdery. *Dehydrated*, the pouch said. But since I didn't have a fire or a pot to cook in, I just sprinkled some on a piece of bread and ate it. Parts of it, like the vegetables, were hard as stones and the noodles were crunchy instead of warm and soft. But—this is how desperate I was—I closed my eyes and savored every bite.

Buddy had two pieces of bread, same as me. Then I took a big swallow of river water from the bottle. Dinner was over.

I was tired of reading the guidebook so I pulled the white card out of my pocket and turned on the little red flashlight. I shone it smack on the "AMBCs" of anger:

A = Activating Event
M = Mind Activity
B = Body Reactions
C = Consequences

Anger. They said that was like my major problem.

I clicked off the light and shoved the card back in my pocket. Didn't need to run down the batteries on that crap.

Darn right I was angry. My father was to blame for all of it, too. True, I still hadn't figured out exactly how I was going to protect my mom and the kids from him. But I'd find something, or something would come to me, I was sure of it.

I rested my head against the brick wall behind me. The river was about a hundred yards away, with rain bouncing off it, creating a gray haze. When lightning flashed I could see two small islands with skinny trees and overgrown bushes halfway across the river. The islands looked like they could've been big animals, like giant water buffaloes wallowing in the river.

That made me think back to the white erase board in Miss Laurie's office, how one day she had drawn a wavy-line river with a blue felt-tip marker and then added these two animals in black, a big-horned antelope standing on shore, and an alligator cruising the water with his mouth open showing off his big, sharp teeth.

"That's the antelope and the alligator," she told me.

"No kidding," I said. "But what's it mean? I mean, why'd you draw it?"

"Well, I'm glad you asked," she said, smiling. And she did have a nice smile. But then she went and told me this little story that made me uncomfortable. She said the antelope on shore was supposed to be me. I was looking across the river at my home. But there was this alligator—my dad—in the water. I had to figure out, she said, how to get home, across the river, while avoiding the alligator.

Get it?

Well, I got it all right. Only I had to shake my head. "Miss Laurie, I don't mean no disrespect, but you don't understand. I spent half my life trying to avoid my dad. But what can you do when you're little and there's no place to hide?"

"Digger, were there any signs of when your dad was about to go off? Did his coming home late mean he'd been drinking? Was that a heads-up?"

"No." I kept shaking my head. "No signs. Nothing like that. My dad didn't work half the time so he didn't have like a regular schedule."

"When he was sober, did you try to talk to him?"

I sat up and looked her in the eye. "You can't talk to my dad. He's like a brick wall. Even if you *think* he's listening, he lives by his own rules and they change every day!"

Miss Laurie frowned, so I gave her an example.

"Okay, look," I said. I tried to explain it to her. "One day my guidance counselor, Mr. Benoit, from my middle school? He came out to my house. This was back in sixth grade. He wanted to talk to my parents about why I'd missed so much school. Was I sick? Was there a family emergency? Well, I was standing there in the kitchen so he could see I wasn't dying from pneumonia or anything.

"My father wasn't there, but my mother sat at the kitchen table. 'No family emergency,' she said. 'He's been helping my husband with work.' But she couldn't go on. She couldn't talk. She leaned her forehead into one of her hands and folded. My mom, she's a good person, really, but she's just not strong when it comes to challenging my dad.

"I spoke up so Mr. Benoit would lay off my mom. I told him the truth—that I had to stay home from school and help my dad haul brush at this construction site 'cause I was being punished.

"He asked me why. 'What did you do? Why were you being punished?'

"My mom and me, our eyes met. I hadn't said anything for years, so why start then? Maybe because I was sick of it, that's why. I was still afraid of my dad, sure. It hurt to get whapped upside the head. But nothing ever got better and I was worried he'd start beating on Hank and LeeAnn.

"'I have to stay home,' I finally told Mr. Benoit, 'on account of I brought home a good report card.'

"Of course he didn't believe it. 'That's crazy!' he said.

"I shrugged. 'My dad said he didn't want no smart-ass son. What he needed was someone to help him get his work done.'

"Well, they got hold of my dad and give him this big lecture about child labor laws and how you couldn't keep a kid out of school like that to make him work, and my dad backed off. I was in class the very next day and my dad never said another word about it. See? You never knew. I think Dad was afraid those Child Protective people from the county would take us kids away. But, like, why would he care?

"Anyway, I never tried as hard in school after that."

Miss Laurie hung on every word I said and I have to admit, it was kind of nice having someone care about what I was saying.

"Here's the kicker," I went on. "I never explained to Mr. Benoit that the whole reason I worked so hard to bring my grades up was to make my dad proud, so maybe he wouldn't be so mean, and so maybe he'd let me go out for basketball. I thought if he went to basketball games at night, he wouldn't drink so much and could sort of be like a normal dad.

"I was dreaming though, wasn't I, Miss Laurie? It's not ever going to happen. He won't change. Some kids, they just don't live in normal families and nothing you say in here can change that."

Miss Laurie was quiet. I mean, I know she said something

to try to make me feel better because that was her job. But really, what could she say that would make a difference? What could she do? What could *anybody* do?

So, as far as I'm concerned, the whole point of the antelope/alligator story is out of whack. Avoiding my old man is *not* the answer, *or* the challenge. Getting *rid* of him was the answer. How to do that was the challenge.

CHAPTER ELEVEN

NEVER AGAIN

A flash of lightning jolted me from sleep. My eyes flew open—just in time to catch sight of the snake coiled up in the leaves near my feet. It had different-colored bands and a yellow tail and sure looked like a copperhead to me!

I froze. I was glad Buddy hadn't seen it yet. Thunder boomed so loud it shook the ground. In another flash of light, I saw the snake raise its head. Yup! That snake's head had a triangle shape to it, which is a huge warning sign that the snake is poisonous.

Slowly I pulled in my feet. At the same time, I reached for the backpack in slow motion. I sure didn't want to deal with a snakebite out in the middle of nowhere.

Gripping the edge of the backpack and holding my breath, I waited for the next flash of light. When it came—and when I saw there wasn't a snake there no more—I grabbed the backpack, yelled "Buddy!" and tore out of there. Thunder boomed as I jumped over a ditch and ran down the trail with the rain pouring down and the dog at my heels.

That snake kept me going a long ways. I ran and walked in the rain for hours that night. All the next day, hiding out again, I was wet, hungry, and just plain miserable. Even after sitting in the sun for a few hours I never got completely dry. Like my underwear was damp and stuck to my skin. I couldn't lie down and get comfortable either. And I was hungry.

I tried to think of other things. Like I saw another beautiful aqueduct, this one over a creek called Antietam, so I read up on it in the guidebook when I stopped to rest. Not far away, there was a big Civil War battle on that creek. Turns out the whole battlefield is still there with cornfields and an old church, even cannons and stuff. A total of twenty-three thousand men died there. When you stop and think about it—that's a lot of people. I wished I'd taken a better look at Antietam Creek when I passed over it. They say the day of the battle that creek ran red with blood.

The same day I crossed Antietam Creek my towpath journey got cut short.

We came to this really beautiful place on the towpath where the Potomac River hooked up with another river called the Shenandoah. A *confluence* it was called, the place where they joined. In between those two rivers at the confluence was a town on a hilly point of land with a lot of people walking around. A bridge went from the town across the river to my side, and to my left, off the towpath, was a steep mountain. I decided Buddy and I would climb up the mountainside to get out of sight and have a good look at things. It was rough going. At times, I had to pull myself up by grabbing on to tree roots and low branches. And a couple times, I had to push Buddy up in front of me.

We finally made it to this rocky ledge with a nice view. Down below, a CSX freight train was coming across the train bridge at a snail's pace and I was close enough to read names on the boxcars: Union Pacific, Burlington Northern, Norfolk Southern. There were huge swirls of graffiti on the boxcars, and in between the slats of the containers, I could see shiny new cars.

After the train passed, I opened the book and found out that long ago this guy named Harper ran a ferry service here so farmers could get their grain to his mill. The town got named for him: Harpers Ferry.

I was getting to be a regular ole annoying history nut, wasn't I? That sure was not my intention. I just didn't have nothing else to do.

Sitting on the rock in the sun, I decided to take off my socks and boots to dry them out some more. Buddy was so beat he lay flat on his side, panting. I put away the guidebook and lay down beside the dog for a short nap.

Right then is when this kid showed up on my rock.

"Hey," he said.

I jumped and sat up.

"Hey," I said back, cussing myself silently at the same time 'cause I knew I should have hid better.

The kid seemed like he was my age. Long, stringy hair fell over part of his face, but his hood was up so it was hard for me to get a good look. He didn't have a backpack or anything, just big, baggy pants and a gray sweatshirt. I looked behind him to see if there was someone with him, but he was alone.

"Mind if I join you?" he asked. His hands were deep in the pockets of those pants that looked like they were gonna fall off any minute.

I shrugged. "Sure. Have a seat."

He did. Right beside me.

"Where you headed?" he asked. "You one of those hikers?" The kid didn't look at me when he asked me this. He faced the river and, like I said, his hood was up, so I couldn't see his face.

"Yeah," I told him. "I'm hiking the towpath down to Georgetown."

"Wow. I guess that's a long way, huh?"

"Pretty long."

"How many miles?"

Was this a test? If I was hiking the whole path then I'd know how many miles total, right? I had to think fast. "It depends on the route you take," I said.

The kid nodded. Guess he didn't realize there was only one route, which meant he wasn't too bright.

"So what's your name?" he asked.

"Gerald," I replied right off. "What's yours?"

The kid turned to me and smirked. "Ronnie," he said.

But I didn't believe him.

"I'm skippin' school," he said as he picked up a stone and shot it downhill.

"Don't worry," I told him, "I won't turn you in."

"Aw, gee. Thanks."

I don't know, was he being sarcastic?

Somehow, we ended up talking about stuff. Like music and movies. I told him some of the things I'd learned about the canal towpath, and he told me about this girl he knew who worked for one of the restaurants across the river in Harpers Ferry. He said she could get us free hamburgers and maybe some fries.

My eyes grew wide. "That would be great," I said. "I am really starved for a hamburger."

"Me too. I gotta wait for her to finish her shift though. Mind if I stretch out on your rock for a bit?"

"No. Suit yourself," I told him.

So he laid back and closed his eyes. I figured it was okay for me to rest a little, too. Maybe dream about that big fat juicy cheeseburger I was gonna get. I'd ask that girl to put onions, catsup, and pickles on it.

Big mistake.

As soon as I closed my eyes that kid grabbed my backpack and took off.

I sprang to my feet, but the hill was steep and rocky and I didn't have my boots on!

"Damn!" I hollered. I slapped my own leg in anger.

Grabbing my boots, I put everything on as fast as I could, then I tore after that kid, stirring up a big cloud of dust as I slipped and slid all the way downhill.

"Go get him!" I yelled at Buddy and pointed. The dog fell down the hill in front of me and charged ahead.

Ten minutes later, I completely lost sight of the boy—and the backpack. When I passed some people on bikes, I asked if they'd seen a kid run by.

"Yes!" a woman told me. She pointed backward with her thumb.

"He stole my backpack," I said.

Another woman pulled out her cell phone. "Should I call the police?"

"No!" I exclaimed, holding up my hands to stop her. "It's okay."

The women seemed confused by that.

"Friend of mine," I blurted. "He's just foolin' around—like he always does. I'll catch up to him. Thanks anyway."

I tried to keep jogging, but I was whipped. I never even saw the rock that tripped me up. Next thing, I'm on the ground, holding my foot and rocking back and forth it hurt so bad. When I tried to stand, I couldn't put any pressure on it. I limped down to the river to get a drink, then took my boot off and stuck my foot in the cold water. I stayed there a long time, soaking my ankle, but it got messed up bad and was already puffy and turning shades of red and purple.

When Buddy returned and sat down beside me, I petted his head. "Thanks for trying," I told him. I had lost everything. With the backpack went the guidebook, the flashlight, the matches, the pancake mix, and the rest of the bread, even the trucker's gray jacket. All I had left were the clothes on my back and the stuff in my pockets: three dollars and a jackknife. I pressed my lips together and shook my head. My own fault. But if I ever caught that kid, he'd be sorry he ran into me.

I found a stick to lean on, like a cane, and when evening came I made my way slowly. By the time I got to another campground, I was totally beat and hid down by the river. I found a spot with a bed of leaves and a rock to prop up my foot. My ankle was so bad then that after I took the boot off, I knew I wouldn't be able to get it back on. So I spent the night there, scratching at bug bites on my face and hugging myself to keep warm. What else could I do? Made me think of this poster in Miss Laurie's office: *Do what you can with what you have where you are.*

But I also started thinking of throwing in the towel and giving myself up. Would I get sent back to Cliffside? How much more time would they give me?

In some ways, I thought, it wouldn't be so bad going back. At least I'd have dry clothes, a bed to sleep in, and three meals a day—plus snacks. Like a granola bar with raisins and nuts, a bowl of buttery popcorn, a shiny apple, a hard-boiled egg with a little salt and pepper sprinkled on it . . .

But then what about Hank and LeeAnn? What about my mom?

I shook my head sadly, torn about what to do and disappointed in myself. I felt dumb I hadn't done this better. At least one thing came out of that mess: I vowed to myself that I would never ever trust anyone again. Not ever.

CHAPTER TWELVE

BLUE LIGHT

All night I lay there with my ankle throbbing like crazy, bug bites itching, and gnats trying to crawl in my eyes. But at least, I thought, I didn't have that blue light shining in my eyes. I had a lot of time that night and all the next day to think about giving myself up and letting my mind drift off to dumb things like that blue light at Cliffside.

It got so I really hated nights at that stinkin' prison. And yeah, it was a prison even if they did call it Cliffside Youth Center on our sweatshirts. In August, when the juvenile court judge sent me and J.T. out to the mountains, she called it a forestry camp, but I don't know where she's been at because it hasn't been a real forestry camp for like seventy years. I saw a picture so I know that a long time ago, during the Great Depression, it was one of those CCC camps President Roosevelt created for guys with no money. They lived at the camp and worked like dogs all day clearing land, building hiking paths, stone walls, stuff like that.

On the wall in the office where we first come in, there's

a framed-up yellowed newspaper picture from back in the 1930s with all those CCC guys piled into the back of a truck with their axes and shovels, heading off to work. Civilian Conservation Corps is what CCC stood for. I'll tell you, I would have much rather worked my butt off like those guys than peel potatoes, analyze my life, and go to school all day, which is mostly what we did.

Anyway, like I said, the nights were bad at Cliffside. There were two dorms, twenty boys in each, and all of us in one big room with tiny windows so high up you couldn't see out. Our beds were jammed together and separated by only a skinny, gray, metal locker, which barely had space for a change of clothes and a toothbrush. We couldn't have anything from home except a couple family pictures, but I didn't have any. Wished I did though. It would have been nice every once in a while to look into little LeeAnn's pretty blue eyes or get a glimpse of my baby brother, Hank, who was growing up so fast. At night sometimes, I'd close my eyes and try to remember what the kids looked like while I settled into that hard, lumpy bed and pulled those scratchy blankets up to my chin. No talking allowed, which was fine with me, so we'd listen to the music they kept on low for a while. WQZK, 94.1 out of Keyser, West Virginia. It was Top 40 stuff, most of it pretty good actually. Supposed to calm us down. I know for a fact some of those guys had tears in their eyes when they finally rolled over and went to sleep.

To my left in that dorm was Abdul, and to my right was Dontaye. I got along okay with both them guys. Abdul was pretty private, but he always said "good night." So did Dontaye, only he talked to me some, too. He was sixteen, which is two years older than me, and hadn't been to school in over a year. We were both at the same math level so sometimes we worked together on homework. I never talked about my family, or my crime, or nothing, but Dontaye spilled out stuff about his life back in Baltimore that made me seriously wonder who had it worse—him or me. He said prison saved him, although I'm sure that didn't mean he liked being there at Cliffside. It seemed like he was way too young to be a dad, but I know he missed his little boy back home. He kept a bent-up picture of his baby son taped inside his locker door and kissed it with his finger every night.

At least Abdul and Dontaye could sleep. In no time, I'd hear 'em both snoring away. Not me. I'd lay there for hours, my hands behind my head, still thinking and worrying about stuff long after the radio got turned off. Even after lights-out the place was never dark 'cause they kept that one blue lightbulb on overhead all the time. Drove me nuts that blue light 'cause it was like somebody staring at me all the time, so I could never really sleep. Boy, do you know what that does to a person?

It was never totally quiet in there either and not just because there was a mouse scratching away in the wall near Abdul's bed. We had this guard, a guy named Joey, in the room with us the entire night, sitting behind his big desk. He wore his leather jacket all the time and he had a vicious case of Dunlap's disease—you know, his stomach *done lapped* over his belt. An old stupid joke, I know, but that was him. He was like an old, stupid joke. A big, fat kid who never grew up. I could hear him fold and unfold the newspaper, but my guess is he only read the comics, if he could read at all. I could hear him clipping his fingernails. I could hear him shuffle and snap cards in place during a game of solitaire. I could hear him rip open his junk food and crunch away on all that stuff he got from the vending machine. Heck, I could even *smell* the guy—like I knew when he got Fritos and when he started in on a pack of them cheese crackers, all of which he washed down with cans of Red Bull. He always left the cans on his desk for us to see in the morning. Like I wondered if he wanted to rub it in our faces that he could use the vending machine and we couldn't.

So, I didn't miss sleeping in that dorm. No way. But here's the weird thing. I was out in the woods, alone. No blue light in my face. No fat guard named Joey keeping an eye out. Still, I had this eerie feeling that someone was watching me.

The next day, I found out who it was.

I hobbled down to the river to get a drink and was throwing sticks for Buddy when I spotted some little fish darting around in the water. Man, I was so hungry I was tempted to reach in and grab a few of them fish to chow down on, but I knew I couldn't catch 'em just like that. So I rigged up a spearlike thing by wrapping the jackknife onto a stick with some vine. I didn't know if it would work—or if I could actually eat raw fish, but I had to try. When this big catfish come along, I stood up and sent that spear flying into the water.

Trouble is that I threw it so hard that the knife came off the stick *and* I lost my balance and fell in.

Big splash. Naturally, the fish got away. I was left soaking wet and feeling like a fool. I pulled the knife out of the sand and was wiping it off with my shirt when I heard someone laugh.

I opened up the big blade on my knife and positioned it tight in my hand. I also picked up a stick from the rock beside me. Slowly, I stood up in the water.

The laughing stopped.

"Who's there?" I demanded.

Buddy barked at the bushes.

"I know you're in there!" I called out.

Unbelievable. But out steps this skinny little kid who was about the same size as my little brother, Hank, who's eight. No kidding. I bet they were the same age only this kid looked like a wimpy little nerd—one of those pale, freckle-faced bookwormy types who couldn't throw a ball or shoot a basket.

The boy seemed scared.

I shushed Buddy and brought down my hand holding the knife.

"I'm not gonna hurt you," the kid said. "Honest."

"Yeah, well, why were you spying on me?"

"I wasn't spying," he said, pushing the glasses up on his nose. His voice got quiet. "I was just watching you. You and your dog . . . What's his name?"

I glanced down at the dog, who stared at my hand, ready to leap the instant I threw the stick. "Buddy," I told him. "His name's Buddy."

"I wish I had a dog like that," the kid said.

I tossed the stick and, while Buddy jumped in the water to fetch it, I sat down on the rock to take the weight off my ankle. While I folded in the blade and slipped the knife back in my pocket, I kept my eyes on the kid. "Who are you?" I asked. "And what are you doing out here?"

"My name's Luke," he said. "Me and my dad, we're staying at the campground."

"Yeah? Is it a big campground? A lot of people?"

"Pretty big. A lot of people."

"Did you tell anyone about me?"

The kid shook his head. "Nobody."

"Well *don't*, okay? I don't want anybody to know I'm here."

"Okay. I promise I won't tell."

I limped out of the water and up onto the riverbank.

"What happened to your foot?" he asked.

"I fell and twisted it. So it's laid me up some. I was hiking the canal path. Me and Buddy. We were doing pretty good until someone stole my backpack."

I swung my head up to look at the kid. "Say, you don't have any food, do you? Like back in your tent?"

His face lit up. "Sure! I can make you a peanut butter sandwich."

"Oh man. I would love it if you could make me a sandwich. I'd take two, in fact—if you can spare the bread. Boy, I would really appreciate it."

Just then, Buddy returned and dropped the stick at my feet.

"And maybe one for Buddy, too?"

"Sure!" He turned to go.

After this kid, Luke, took off, I wondered what I should do. Whether I should get going before he came back with someone, or just hide to see if he came back alone with those peanut butter sandwiches. I was pretty hungry.

I stood and threw the stick again for Buddy, then touched my puffy black and blue ankle and sat down. I wasn't ready to give up after all, and I was thinking if I could get some food we'd travel at night again. Even if I did have to limp along, we'd take it slow and work our way down the towpath.

Sitting there waiting, however, I felt something sticky and made a discovery that was going to change my plans. Those bug bites on my face? They weren't bug bites. They were poison ivy blisters oozing all around my eyes, down my cheeks, and across my nose. I had it on my arms and hands, too. Damn, I thought. I must've picked it up when I was lying in the woods that second night out.

Soon, the kid was back—*alone*—and with a plastic bag full of food! Four peanut butter sandwiches, plus a couple bananas and two cans of Coke.

I scarfed down two of them sandwiches right away while the kid fed pieces of another one to Buddy. Then I popped the top on a can of soda and drained it without stopping. I split the fourth sandwich between me and Buddy and then sat there peeling a banana.

"Boy, I really appreciate this," I said around a mouthful. "If I had a bunch of money I'd pay you for it, but like I said I got ripped off."

Luke shrugged. "It's okay. My dad won't mind."

I stopped eating. "Your dad? Did you tell him it was for me?"

The boy shook his head. "My dad's not even here. He doesn't get home from work until almost dinnertime."

"He's working while you're on vacation?"

"We're not on vacation," Luke said. "We *live* here."

"I thought you said this was a campground."

"It *is*! But a lot of people, they live here. Some people got giant RVs and stuff. My dad and me sleep in a big tent. It's nice though. We got cots and a rug on the floor. We even have a little TV that runs on batteries. Some people, they sleep on the ground. And these two guys we know, Jeff and Kyle, they sleep in their car. They smoke pot, too. We can smell it."

"Wow," I said, and kind of rolled my eyes.

I finished off both bananas while Luke babbled away about himself. I found out he was in the third grade, just like Hank, that he liked math, but was no bookworm 'cause he hated to read. He said he wanted a dog like mine someday, and he bragged about his rock collection, which sounded pretty lame to me. After a while Luke said he needed to get back to do his homework. I figured I wouldn't see the kid again so I thanked him a second time for the food and wished him good luck.

After he left, I took a couple napkins he'd brought, dipped them in the cold river water, and pressed them against the poison ivy on my face. Even though I'd eaten, I didn't feel so great. I went back to where I'd been lying down and stretched out with the damp napkins stuck to my face and my foot up on the rock. My face itched so bad I felt like I wanted to scratch if off, but I fell asleep anyway and slept clear through the night.

Next thing I knew birds were singing. I smelled a wood fire, probably from the campground, and I heard a couple vehicles start up and leave. Sunlight coming through the trees started to warm my face and made it more itchy. Then I had that weird blue light feeling again, like someone was watching me. Only this time I couldn't do a thing about it, or even know for sure 'cause—this was *really* scary—I couldn't *see* anything. The poison ivy had made my eyes swell up and close.

CHAPTER THIRTEEN

TOO GOOD TO BE TRUE

"Do you think he's dead?"

"No. Watch his stomach. It moves when he breathes. See? He's not dead. Why would he be dead?"

"I don't know. I mean he was starving to death yesterday."

"Well, he's alive all right."

"What do you think we should do?"

Lying there, pretending to be asleep underneath those napkins on my face, I felt Buddy beside me lift his head. I recognized Luke's voice right off. The other voice belonged to a girl.

"I think he's in trouble because he didn't want me to say anything to my dad about finding him, or making him those sandwiches," Luke said. "What do you think he did?"

"Who knows?" The girl sounded older than Luke.

"Do you think he robbed a store? Or maybe he killed somebody!"

"Nah." The girl was doubtful. "He doesn't look like a killer."

A sudden heaviness sank into my chest. If she only knew.

"But it's none of our business, right?" The girl's voice.

"Right," Luke agreed.

"So we ought to help him."

"Yeah. He seemed kind of nice—I mean he was good to his dog."

"You can tell a lot about a person from the way they treat their animals. Go ahead, Luke, wake him up."

Their slow, careful footsteps crunched through the leaves.

Buddy's tail started going back and forth, whacking me on one leg.

"This dog is named Buddy," Luke whispered to the girl.

"How original," she said.

"Hey, Buddy, it's okay. It's me, Luke. Remember? I fed you a sandwich yesterday." Buddy stood up. "Good boy. How are ya?"

Suddenly, Luke's voice was close to my ear: "Hey, mister, are you okay? We worried you died or something."

I snorted, and I couldn't help but grin.

"See, I told you he was alive!" the girl exclaimed.

I pushed myself up, peeled the napkins off my face, and leaned back on my elbows. "Yeah, I'm alive, but I can't see. The poison ivy made my eyes swell shut." As I said this, however, I discovered that I could actually get a glimpse of the world through two tiny slits.

The girl stood behind Luke. She looked like a teenager, someone my age. She smelled nice, too. I got a big whiff of her perfume, or whatever it was.

"Ewww!" she said as she came closer.

"Nora! Don't touch him 'cause then you'll get it, too!"
Luke warned.

"No, I won't," the girl declared. "You can't *catch* poison ivy
from someone else. It's not contagious like that."

"I got it from my dad once," Luke claimed.

"Was it the first time you ever had poison ivy?" she asked.
"If it was, that's why. It takes longer for your body to react the
very first time you get it. You and your dad probably picked it
up at the same time."

"All I know is that it's all over these woods," Luke said.

"It's so much worse now, too, because of global warming.
There's more carbon dioxide in the air and poison ivy thrives
on it—"

"Hey, I hate to interrupt the lecture on poison ivy," I said,
"but can you guys help me?"

"We can try," the girl said. "What you need is a shower.
Then give me your clothes and I'll throw them away."

I sat all the way up. "What are you talking about? I can't
throw away my clothes! They're all I got!"

"But the oil from the poison ivy is all over them by now.
It'll keep reinfecting you. That oil can last up to a year."

"Can't I just wash it out?"

"Probably not," the girl said.

I moaned. Throwing away my clothes seemed extreme.
Plus I didn't have anything else to wear.

"I'm telling you, that's what you need to do," she said. She
was starting to sound like a Miss Know-It-All. "You should've
been careful: *Leaves of three, leave me be.*"

"Hey, I *know* what poison ivy looks like!" I snapped back.

"So as soon as you touched it you should have found some jewelweed and rubbed it all over. It's the natural antidote to poison ivy, you know."

Jewelweed? I didn't know what she was talking about.

"I slept in the woods one night," I declared. "It was dark. I couldn't see. That's probably when I got it!"

She chuckled. "Looks like you've spent more than one night in the woods!"

Guess that meant I looked pretty bad. And maybe smelled ripe, too. This girl was beginning to irritate me. "Yeah, well, someone stole all my stuff."

She grunted. "I don't know if you're stupid, or just plain pathetic."

I didn't answer 'cause I guess I didn't know either. I lay back down.

Next thing, the girl's voice softened up. "All right, *okay*. If you want our help, we can guide you up to the showers." She must've turned to Luke. "Run back to your tent and get him some clothes. Like a pair of your dad's sweatpants or some shorts, and a T-shirt, something like that."

"His *dad's* clothes?" I didn't think that was such a great idea.

"Yeah, I think his stuff would fit you," she said.

I didn't want to argue with her. I was miserable and let's face it, I needed the help.

Nora and Luke guided me to the campground bathhouse. There was some leftover soap in one of the shower stalls so

Luke led me into that one. I pulled the plastic curtain shut, undressed, and dropped my clothes outside the shower stall. I soaped up good and took a long hot and cold shower (hot and cold because the water kept changing). It was the first shower I'd had in several days and I have to say, it felt good.

Meanwhile, Luke got me some clothes: a pair of what Nora described as "ugly plaid shorts," some boxers, and a white T-shirt. Everything was a little big, but I wasn't complaining. Luke also brought me a towel and a pair of his dad's flip-flops 'cause Nora had put my boots in a plastic bag and said she was going to wipe them down with alcohol, which, according to her, was about the only way to get rid of the poison ivy oil.

This was weird: after I dried off, Luke gave me a paper cup full of a paste Nora made with baking soda and water and told me to spread it all over the poison ivy. It was goopy, but you know what? It stopped me from itching so bad.

I could hear Buddy barking outside the bathhouse while I finished up. Then I heard a man's voice. I should've known the kids would go get an adult. I hesitated in the doorway, struggling to see, and wondered if I'd done myself in.

"Name's Sherwood Hawkins, but everybody calls me Woody," this guy said. He touched me on the shoulder and kind of squeezed it. "My son, Luke, here, says you could use some help."

I couldn't see the guy so there was no way to size him up other than his voice, which sounded normal. I dropped my head. "Yeah. I could use some help."

"What's your name, son?"

"Gerald," I told him, using the same fake name I'd used earlier.

"Do they call you Gerry?" Woody asked.

"Yeah. Gerry. They call me Gerry," I lied.

"Is there someone you need to call?" he asked. "Like your—"

"No!" I cut him off. "Nobody. I'm on my own now."

He didn't press the issue.

Woody had me sit down on a stump and felt around my ankle like he knew what he was doing, then he wrapped it up in an Ace bandage. "I wouldn't put any weight on that foot for a while," he advised.

I nodded. The tight wrap felt good. "Thanks."

"Luke said you had your backpack stolen, so why don't you come over to our site? I've got a pup tent. Luke and I can pitch it for you and you can stay there for a couple days. I've got an air mattress and I'm sure we can find an extra blanket. You're welcome to join us for dinner, too. Nothing fancy, mind you. Hot dogs and beans tonight."

A warm meal sounded great. So did an air mattress and a blanket.

"I'd be grateful," I said. "Maybe just until I get my eyesight back."

"*And* until that ankle heals up," Woody suggested.

At their campsite, Woody and Luke pitched the tent, pumped up that air mattress, and gave me a set of sheets, a couple blankets, and a pillow. There was room for only one person in the tent, but enough space for Buddy to curl up beside me. Woody gave me a couple Advil with a glass of water, then I stretched out before I even made up my bed and fell dead asleep until they called me for dinner. Hot dogs and beans, a piece of bread, iced tea, and a big chunk of watermelon for dessert. A feast, if you ask me. It tasted great, all of it. Even Buddy had hot dogs for dinner.

The next couple days, I stayed in the old, orange pup tent beside Luke and his dad in the bigger green tent. I was on edge about it, 'cause I didn't know those people from Adam. But I guess I was more tired than I was worried 'cause I slept most of the time. Other times though, I just lay there with my eyes closed, listening to the campground sounds. They had a rhythm. Like in the morning, I'd hear voices and coughs, twigs snapping and wood-chopping noises as people got their fires going. I'd hear the slap of that screen door down to the bathhouse and the sound of cars and trucks starting up and driving off. Then it would grow quiet for a while. Several times a day a train rumbled by not far away and once, a garbage truck came through. Guess I knew *that* sound pretty well. Late in the afternoon, I'd hear people coming back, more voices—more kids' voices, and the creak of a metal chain, like on a swing.

After Luke and his dad got home, I'd listen in on their conversations. Like I heard Luke call his dad once to get a spider and another time to say he had the checkerboard ready. I heard Woody ask if Luke got his homework done and then a while later Luke singsong "King me! King me!" I heard Woody say "Don't forget your toothbrush" when they headed off to the bathhouse. And both nights, I listened as Woody read Luke parts of a story called *Burt Dow, Deep-Water Man*. Seems ole Burt had a leaky boat called the *Tidely-Idley* and every time Woody come to that name he must've tickled Luke 'cause the giggling started all over again.

Buddy came and went, although he never went far. Every once in a while I took off the Ace bandage. Luke filled little bags of ice for my ankle and Woody gave me a bottle of pink calamine lotion to put on the poison ivy with cotton balls. In the mornings, they brought me breakfast—usually a bowl of cereal and a cup of bitter, black coffee. Then Luke left me with two peanut butter and jelly sandwiches before he went to catch the bus for school. Woody said I was welcome to Coke and water from their cooler. Evenings, I had whatever dinner they had.

By the third day, my eyes were much better, but my ankle was still tender so I hopped over and sat at the picnic table to have a look around. I could see it was a big campground with all kinds of RVs and tents. Each campsite had a picnic table and a stone fireplace with a built-in grill. A spigot for water was just down the road, but no electric hookups. I saw a playground down the road and noticed it had a basketball court, but Luke didn't have a ball.

With my eyesight back, I also saw Woody had blond hair like Luke, a beard, and small, kind of slanted brown eyes that reminded me of a fox. His neck, face, and hands were red from the sun on account of the construction work he did. When he got home he was always sweaty and really beat so as soon as I was up and moving around I pitched in making dinner. Luke and me, we started cooking as soon as Woody eased his pickup into the campsite and popped open his first can of beer.

Our dinners were pretty simple: hot dogs and macaroni from the box, bologna sandwiches, hamburgers. One time, Woody brought home some tomatoes and we made BLTs. Another time, we didn't find much of anything in the two plastic food bins so we made up some pancakes and eggs.

Just when I thought we plumb run out of food, Woody showed up with six bags of groceries—and a brand-new basketball.

I don't know. I was grateful and I was rolling with it, but I kept remembering that saying: *If something is too good to be true, then it probably is.*

CHAPTER FOURTEEN

THIS GIRL, NORA

After my eyesight cleared up, I also had a good look at this girl, Nora. First thing I noticed is that she was pretty. Plus she had a nice figure, which I was very aware of because her jeans were skintight and her tank top clinged to every nice curve she had. Her hair was long and shiny black—except for a single stripe of blue. She liked to twist and drape her long hair over one shoulder. Her bangs were long, too, and hid the tops of her eyes, making her seem kind of mysterious.

Different. That's a word you would definitely use to describe Nora. Besides being pretty, she had a tiny silver stud on one side of her nose, a rose tattoo on her upper right arm, and she wore blue eyeliner that matched the stripe in her hair. She looked sort of punk, but she didn't act weird like some of the punk girls I knew back in middle school.

True, she did still have an annoying, I'm-better-than-you attitude but maybe 'cause she was so smart. She took all college prep classes at the local high school where she was a freshman (which is what I'd be if I hadn't been sent off to

Cliffside). And the second day she ever talked to me she told me she was going to be a doctor. I couldn't understand then why she'd want to waste her time coming to see me every afternoon after school, but I'm glad she did. One day, she brought over my boots, which she had cleaned so thoroughly they looked like new. Another day she brought me a pair of crutches 'cause I was still hobbling around.

"So how do you like Woody?" she asked one afternoon. She and I were sitting at the picnic table waiting for Luke to finish his homework in the tent. When he was done we were going to walk down to the river to go fishing.

"Woody?" I looked across the table at her, but hesitated saying anything because I still wasn't sure what to think about him—*or* about Nora.

"Well, one thing's for sure," I said. "He's a good dad. Every night, he and Luke have a game of checkers, then they read a book together." I kind of shook my head like in disbelief. "My father never once read me a book."

Nora kind of snorted. "Yeah. I don't even *have* a dad!"

"What do you mean?"

"I mean I know I *have* a dad," Nora went on, "but I've never met him. He lives down South somewhere. Mom said he already had a family when he met her. He paid my mom a bunch of money to go away. He'd probably have a heart attack if I showed up on his doorstep one day. Believe me, I've thought about it. . . .

"Anyway, you're right that Woody really does love Luke," she continued, "but there's something else about Woody I haven't figured out yet. I babysat for Luke this summer and, I don't know, sometimes I had these weird vibes. If I were you, I'd be careful about getting too involved."

She looked at me like she wanted me to agree with her. But so far, Woody had been nothing but kind to me. Plus I didn't plan on sticking around so I wasn't worried about getting too involved. I just shrugged. "Okay," I told her. "Thanks. I'll be careful."

A pause.

"So you live with your mom then?" I asked her.

"Yeah. We've lived here a few months 'cause it's inexpensive. I mean, some people are here on a vacation, sure, but a lot of people live here because it's cheaper than renting an apartment and paying utilities."

"Utilities?"

"You know, like gas and electric?"

"Ah." I didn't volunteer the information that we'd had the electric cut off at my house a bunch of times when my parents didn't pay the bill.

"A lot of people here have seasonal jobs," Nora explained. "Picking vegetables or doing construction. My mom works at a horse farm."

Nora pushed a pen and a napkin toward me across the picnic table and I saw that she had drawn a tic-tac-toe grid on it.

"A horse farm?"

"She's a trainer. I work there on the weekends with her. You could get a part-time job there, too, if you wanted. They always need people to muck stalls."

I put an *o* in the tic-tac-toe grid. "Muck stalls?"

"You know, shoveling manure, pitching hay. It pays minimum wage."

"How much is that?"

Nora added an *x*. "I think minimum wage is seven twenty-five right now."

My head sprang up in surprise. "An hour?"

When Nora nodded I thought, wow. If I worked an eight-hour day that would be like fifty-eight dollars a day. Quickly, I placed an *o*.

"Would I have to give somebody an ID?"

"I don't think so," she said. "The woman who runs the farm is super nice. Now that her summer volunteers are gone, she really needs the help."

Nora made her next move and I made mine.

"Got ya!" Nora exclaimed as she added a third *x* and drew a diagonal line through the grid.

While she drew up a new game, my mind was spinning. It would be nice to make a little bit of money. I could work there while Luke was in school, or on weekends. And working at a farm would be safe. I could pretty much keep out of sight. But this was the other thing: farms had all kinds of stuff lying around. At my grandfather's farm, my friends and I once discovered a rusted sword in the upper hayloft. It was on a windowsill, up high where the pigeons flew in. Grampa didn't have a clue where it come from. Not only that, but we ran across rat poison, old containers of kerosene, cattle prods, shotgun shells, all kinds of dangerous stuff. I would need some kind of weapon if I was gonna protect my mom and the kids when I got home. Maybe I'd find it at this farm.

"All done!" Luke exclaimed as he came from the tent with his tackle box in hand. I put the horse farm job in the back of my mind, and we three set off for the river. Luke ran ahead with Buddy, while Nora carried the fishing rod and walked slowly beside me as I hobbled on the crutches.

Another hot day. When we got down to the river I was sweating. "You and Luke ought to jump in and take a swim," I suggested to Nora. "If I didn't have this sprained ankle, that's what I'd do."

Nora wrinkled her nose. "Nah. I don't want to get my hair wet. Besides, Luke can't swim."

"No kidding." Having grown up near a river myself, I never knew a kid who couldn't swim.

I helped Luke get a fly on the end of his hook, then Nora and I sat on two nearby rocks. We watched Luke cast out and reel in.

"Slow!" I called out to Luke. "Don't reel it in so fast. You gotta give those fish time to see your bait. You want that fish to think that spinner is a worm or a bug. What you're trying to do is trick the fish."

Right off, Luke started reeling in more slowly. "Like this?" he called out.

"Yup!" I gave him a thumbs-up.

Nora smiled. "He likes you."

I smiled, too. Then stupid me, I blurted out, "Back home I have a brother the same age, and a little sister, too."

Nora didn't seem to catch the look on my face. "You're lucky," she said. "I don't have a brother or a sister. It's just me and my mom. I mean, we're really close and all. But I think it would be nice to have a sister to talk to sometimes. We move around so much it's hard for me to make friends."

"You don't have friends at school?"

She shook her head. "I don't *want* friends at school!"

"I thought everybody wanted friends."

"Not me!" she said. "I don't let anybody at the high school get close. I don't want them to know I live at the campground because then they'd write me off. *And* probably give me grief about it."

She was quiet, then added, "So if you ever *don't* want friends, just do something really weird with your hair or else pierce your nose. People leave you alone when you're different enough. A tattoo here and there doesn't hurt either. Shows people you're tough."

I felt like I should've said something to her then. I punched out kids plenty of times so they'd leave me alone. And I knew what it was like to have to hide something. But if I told her stuff, how'd I know what she would do with that information? Undecided, I just sat there again saying nothing while another whole minute went by. I watched Luke casting in and out.

"So," Nora said, "who is Michael Griswald?"

"What?" I swung my head around fast.

"Michael Griswald," she said, repeating my name.

My mouth fell open. Like how'd she know?

"Here," she said, not waiting for me to come up with an

answer. "You left this card in the pocket of those pants I threw away. I forgot to give it to you."

It was the white card from Cliffside. I forgot about the card! And the fact it had my name on it. Although she had no way of knowing it was *my* name.

"I—I don't know what this is," I said, letting her place the card in my hand. I was dumbstruck. Only thing that card didn't have on it was where I'd been. Like it didn't say juvenile detention center or anything like that.

"I saw it lying on the towpath and picked it up," I told her.

She reached into her pocket and pulled out some folded dollar bills and a little bit of loose change. "Here," she said, handing me the cash I'd taken from the truck driver. She dug into her other pocket. "Oh, and this jackknife."

I couldn't believe I'd forgotten those things! I tried to study Nora's face. Like did she suspect anything? What was she going to do? But I couldn't tell 'cause all at once she stood up and brushed off her shorts.

"I've got to get back and do some homework," she said.

I was totally speechless and sat there staring at the stuff in my hands until it sunk in that she was leaving.

"Hey! Thanks again for the crutches!" I called after her.

"Sure thing," she replied. And she waved, but without turning around.

CHAPTER FIFTEEN

THE OTHER SHOE

Besides making dinner with Luke, I was also helping him with his homework. The math was easy for him, but reading was another story. My little brother, Hank, could read a whole lot better than Luke. I also got Luke started with some exercises to build himself up. He said he wanted to be like me and I guessed that meant he wanted some muscles like I got from doing all those pull-ups on the rusty swing set back home. "We'll train like the Marines," I told him.

"Is that what you're going to be? A Marine?" Luke asked.

"I hope so."

"How come?"

"'Cause Marines are tough," I said. "Nobody messes with a Marine."

"I want to be a Marine, too!"

I laughed. "We've got a lot of work to do then!"

One day, when Woody got off work early, he suggested we drive into town and get me some clothes at the Goodwill store.

"But I don't have any money," I said. Plus I was anxious about being seen.

Woody shrugged it off. "Don't matter. It won't cost much at the Goodwill."

I didn't protest 'cause I needed something that fit right and looked better than those baggy plaid shorts. No way was I going to wear those shorts down to the basketball court when my ankle got better.

We three squeezed into the front seat of Woody's pickup. It was my first time out of the campground since I came. Soon after we left it we drove over a set of railroad tracks so I saw where the trains come through. The town wasn't much farther away, but there wasn't much in Harwick—a bar, a pizza joint, a gas station, and a bunch of old buildings, some that looked lived in and some that didn't. Luke pointed to a church and told me it was a coffee shop now called Holy Grounds, which I thought was pretty funny. You know, *coffee* grounds, *holy* grounds . . . Besides coffee, Luke said, the café had computers that kids used after school.

At the Goodwill store, I hobbled up and down the aisles on my crutches. We picked up two pairs of jeans, a couple T-shirts, a long-sleeved shirt, and a Washington Redskins sweatshirt. I'm not a Redskins fan. I root for the Ravens. But it's not like there was a big choice or anything. It only cost about ten bucks for all that stuff. I told Woody I'd work to repay him but he waved his hand at me. When he went to the food store, he even bought Buddy a big bag of dog food. And later, when he gave me two packs of new boxers and socks, a toothbrush, and a stick of deodorant, he shook his head again and said, "Don't worry about it."

But I did worry. He must've known I couldn't repay him. So I wondered why he was being so nice. I mean, part of me was *still* waiting for the other shoe to drop.

The next evening, after we had shared a pizza at the picnic table and Luke went to bed, Woody and me sat in the two flimsy beach chairs around the fire we'd made, in part to keep the bugs away.

"How's the ankle?" he asked.

"Still hurts a little, but not bad," I said.

"I sure hope you didn't break a bone or nothin'."

"Nah, I don't think so. Just a sprain."

Then Woody asked, "So what are you runnin' from?"

I tried to be cool. "What? You think I'm a runaway?"

"Course I do," he said. "You don't look a day older than fourteen or fifteen. I figure you're either runnin' *from* something, or *to* something. Ain't my business to know what. But I'll tell you this, Gerry—if that's your name—I do understand. I run away from home myself when I was sixteen. Never went back neither."

I didn't say anything. I didn't want to confide in him, but I didn't want to lie any more than I had to either. Cautious, I looked up at him.

"Don't worry," Woody said. "I ain't gonna turn you in."

I stayed silent. Woody stared into the fire.

"Quite frankly, I'm glad you're here," he went on. Then he looked at me. "I like you. And I appreciate you helpin' Luke with dinner and homework. Glad, too, that you're here when he gets home from school. So it seems a fair enough trade for me. You sleepin' and eatin' here. I feel like I can trust you to take care of Luke until I get home."

I gave him a slight nod.

"Think I can do that?" he asked. "Trust you?"

I couldn't help but remember Nora's warning to be careful of getting too involved. But really, it did seem fair. I'd have a place to sleep and three squares a day in exchange for taking care of Luke.

"Sure," I agreed. "It's the least I can do for all the help you give me."

We went to bed soon after that. But I would think back on that conversation for a couple reasons: one, 'cause Woody suspected the truth about me running, and two, on account of the fact that the very next day, the other shoe dropped.

What happened is that without a word, note, or phone call to anyone, Woody simply didn't come home from work.

I mean, the day started out like all the others. In the morning when I got up, Woody was already gone. So I had a dish of cereal with Luke and got myself a cup of coffee. I offered to make Luke a sandwich but he said he got free lunch at school. "I didn't want it, but Dad said I had to take it," he mumbled.

"Hey, I know how you feel," I told him. "I was on free lunch for years."

"You were?"

"Yup. Free breakfast, too."

Luke kind of frowned and glanced at me. "Weren't you embarrassed?"

I shrugged. "Maybe—in the beginning. But I wasn't the only one in that corner of the cafeteria every morning. I was grateful for that food."

"You were? How come?"

I shrugged. "Sometimes for dinner at home, all I had to eat was Goldfish!"

Luke's eyes got wide. "What? Those little crackers?"

I nodded. "Yup."

Then I cut off the conversation and told him he'd better hurry or he'd miss the bus.

The whole routine reminded me of Hank and LeeAnn. Normally, I'd be gone to school before them, but if Mom and Dad were either not home, or not functioning, I'd be the one to get the kids up and out of there. Hank and LeeAnn shared bunk beds, and I'd have to reach up and practically roll Hank out of the top one. He was deadweight that time of the morning. I'd find clothes, sometimes dirty ones off the floor, and then walk them out to the road to wait for the bus. They whined a lot, like how come I could stay home, but they couldn't. But I was tough. I always figured they were better off at school than at home. Plus they'd get breakfast—lunch, too—and on Fridays, I knew their teachers would stuff granola bars and little cereal boxes in their backpacks for the weekend.

After Luke left, I straightened up the campsite a little. I

put the milk away in the cooler and threw the paper bowls we used for cereal in the trash. The spoons we ate with went in a little plastic tub. Every once in a while we took the tub to the bathhouse, Luke and me, to wash everything in the sink where there was hot water.

I went into the big tent to toss Luke's slippers by his bed and while I was there I set my crutches down and sat on his cot to rest a minute. Luke slept in a sleeping bag, but he had smoothed it out and zipped it up all neat with his floppy stuffed tiger tucked in at the pillow. He had a milk crate tipped on its side by his cot for a night table. On top was an old-fashioned windup clock that ticked really loud, a box of Kleenex, a smooth white rock he found at the river, and a cup of water he'd had overnight. Inside the crate, at the bottom, was the book Woody had read to him last night and, beside it, a framed picture facedown. I picked it up and saw it was a picture of Luke when he was maybe three or four years old, being hugged by a woman with a lot of freckles and thick, curly red hair. This is funny: they both wore cowboy hats. I took a closer look. That woman's eyes— and her nose—looked like Luke's. I wondered if it was Luke's mom and, if so, where she was.

I set the picture down the way I found it and returned to my tent thinking about my own mother. I hadn't forgotten her, or the kids. But I knew I couldn't get far down the path on crutches, plus I'd stick out like a sore thumb with my poison ivy. I needed to chill for a while. And let's face it, with Luke and his dad, I had a pretty good thing going at that camp. Except that now, a whole day had gone by, and Woody hadn't come home. It was after six o'clock and usually, he got home around four. I knew Woody had a cell phone, but Luke didn't so how could he call us?

"Is your dad ever late like this?" I asked Luke as we gathered some sticks to make a fire.

"Sometimes," he said.

"So you never know?"

Luke shook his head.

Boy, I could identify with that. Parents gone. No word on who was where.

After we had a fire going under the grill, I cooked cheese sandwiches in a frying pan for supper. Then we toasted a couple marshmallows on sticks for dessert. While we were pulling them off, all drippy and gooey, Nora showed up. She had her hair all twisted up into a pretty ponytail bun kind of thing.

"Hey, I wondered if you guys wanted to come into town with my mom and me," she said. "She's going to drop me off at Holy Grounds Café so I can use the Internet. It's air-conditioned in there and they have a lot of comfy couches. Luke could get his homework done and it would be a change of scenery for you."

"Can we, Gerry? Can we?" Luke asked eagerly. "I have some money Dad left me, so we could get something at the snack bar."

"You do?" I wondered how much more money he had.

When he disappeared into the tent to get the money I told Nora that Woody hadn't come home from work yet. "I'm not sure we should go. Besides, don't you think my face will freak everybody out?"

She giggled. "I don't think so. I mean it looks bad, yeah—"

"Oh, thanks!"

"But it's obvious it's just poison ivy," she insisted.

"*Just?*"

"You know what I mean. It's not like you have the plague or anything."

I grinned. "But maybe I should call Woody. Do you have his number?"

"No!" Nora said right away. "I don't have his number. And besides, my cell phone's not charged."

No big deal, I thought. I decided we'd go. Having been in Harwick once before I wasn't too concerned about being seen by many people. I did worry a little about Buddy, but we'd left him at the camp before and he was all right. Besides, I couldn't let the dog rule my life.

With a piece of paper I tore from Luke's notebook, I left a note for Woody under the big citronella candle on the picnic table.

Nora's mom pulled up in a little red Chevy missing its front bumper and, from the sounds of it, part of the muffler, too. Nora piled into the backseat with Luke so I could have more room with my crutches in the front seat.

"Hi there!" Her mother shook my hand. She was a small woman, but since she was wearing a sleeveless top I could see she had muscular arms and a lot of tattoos—horses and flowers mostly. "My name's Miranda."

"I'm Gerry," I had to tell her.

When she dropped us off, she said she'd be back in a couple hours, that she was just running over to the Walmart in Charles Town, which was in West Virginia. That sounded far, but she said it was ten minutes away.

It was nice in the old church coffeehouse. The air-conditioning was really cranked up and it felt great 'cause we'd had a streak of hot weather despite it being fall. But it killed me to see Luke pay so much money for the snacks they sold. Most of it was high-class kind of stuff like scones and shortbread and muffins the size of a grapefruit. Luke bought a huge chocolate chip cookie which we split, and two lemonades, which used up half of that twenty.

While Nora started piling her books on one of the tables, I checked them out. She was taking American history and biology, and she was already in algebra II. There was also a white book called *Vocabulary for the College-Bound Student*. I felt a twinge seeing those books. Guess 'cause I should have been in school, too. Maybe not with college prep classes, but at least so I'd graduate.

"Come on, Gerry," Luke said, tugging me over to a nearby couch.

He whispered, "This story is called *Walking on a Wire*. You read it first, Gerry, then me."

Gerry. Boy, every time I heard that name I felt weird.

We put the book between us on a pillow and I pointed to the words as I read quietly: "In 2001, the Wallenda family did something that had never been done before. First, four men in the family stood on a wire high in the air. Then they held poles between them." I finished the other four sentences in the paragraph ending with this line: "They made a pyramid of eight people, all standing on a wire!

"Your turn," I said, taking my hands away.

But Luke didn't want to read the next paragraph. Instead, he tried to read the same paragraph I had read—only he couldn't get past the first sentence.

"In 2001, the Wa . . .Wa . . ."

"Wallenda," I told him.

"In 2001, the Wallenda family did something that had never been done before . . ."

"Go ahead," I urged him. "First, four men . . ."

Luke pushed the glasses up on his nose. "First, four men . . ."

"In the family."

"In the family," he repeated.

I had to help again: "Stood on a wire."

"Stood on a wire," he echoed. Then he read the entire line again. "First, four men in the family stood on a wire." After which he repeated the title of the story, *Walking on a Wire*, and the first two lines a second time.

I rolled my eyes 'cause I realized it was going to take us a very long time to get through this story.

When we finally finished, I told Luke to do his math while I sat at an unused computer and went online for fun. Well, actually not for fun. What I wanted to do was check to see if there were any articles about my escape. I googled "youth prison escape Maryland." And up popped a story from a couple days ago:

JUVENILE ESCAPES FROM YOUTH DETENTION CENTER

CUMBERLAND—Authorities continued their search for a fourteen-year-old boy who escaped from the Cliffside Youth Detention Center ten days ago. They speculate the boy either walked off the property and was picked up or, possibly, that he fled by hiding in a garbage truck. According to state police, the boy may have hijacked a tractor-trailer rig parked at a diner on I-68 and then abandoned the vehicle at a runaway truck ramp on the east side of Sideling Hill.

"He's a wily character, for sure," said State Police Sergeant Dean Cropper. He noted that the abandoned truck had caught fire from burning brakes and was damaged extensively.

Police have posted notices throughout the state and are searching the nearby C&O Canal towpath, which may have provided an escape route. Authorities also continued to stake out the boy's home on the Eastern Shore . . .

I had to look away for a moment. If police were staking out my house then I couldn't go home. There was more to that article, but I didn't finish reading it because just then in walked two cops! Clearly, they were looking around.

My heart beat double time because suddenly I realized this whole thing—us coming into town—was a setup!

I shot a glance at Nora, who pretended to be busy with her schoolwork.

When the cops walked toward the refreshment counter, I picked up my crutches. They hadn't spotted me yet. Then I left—just as quickly as I could.

CHAPTER SIXTEEN

LOCKED IN

At first I thought I'd hide in the bathroom, but then I figured that was too obvious. So when I saw this other door, with steps leading down, I went that way instead. When I closed the door I heard it latch behind me. I tried opening it, just to see if I could, but it was locked solid.

It was pitch black with the door shut. I set down my crutches, sat on the top step, and started easing myself down slowly, only to discover that after four steps there was a wall. I wasn't going anywhere.

I shook my head, disgusted at myself for trusting that girl. But then I wondered: Why'd she bother to give me the white card back? Why tell me about that job at the horse farm? Why bring me into town? Why not just have the cops come out to the campground?

These questions didn't have answers. I sat, frozen in the dark, feeling my stomach twist itself into a big knot.

More questions flooded my brain. What did the word *wily* mean? That state police guy said I was a *wily* character.

What would happen if they found me? The boys back at Cliffside would get a big kick out of my poison ivy, wouldn't they? Tio would say something nasty right off and I'd have to punch him out for it.

My mouth went dry while my mind kept jumping around. Would I ride out to Cliffside handcuffed? How many more months—or years—would they tack on to my sentence for running? Who'd take care of Buddy? And Luke?

I heard people walk past the door. I thought I heard boots clunk past. Those cops were wearing boots. A police radio crackled. "On our way," someone said.

Had I made a mistake? Did I jump to the wrong conclusions? If so, it would be really embarrassing to call out for help.

Meanwhile, I was locked in and that was making me break out into a cold sweat. I didn't like being locked in. Not one bit. I rubbed the moist palms of my hands on my leg.

I shifted position. I wiped a hand over my mouth. I glanced back at the door. What was I going to do?

When I heard Nora's voice, I quickly pushed myself back up the four steps and leaned toward the crack in the door so I could hear.

"Go in the men's room and look," she said. A few seconds later: "No? Well, go back and sit down, Luke. I'll check outside."

Footsteps. Luke walking away?

"Nora!" I said in a low voice. "Psssst . . . Nora!"

"Gerry?! Where are you?"

She must've turned around then and seen the other door.

She tried the knob, but the door didn't budge. She tried harder and it popped open, like it had been stuck, not locked. Boy, I felt like a real idiot then.

"What are you doing in there?" Nora exclaimed.

"Shhhhh!" I grabbed her by the arm, pulled her in, and closed the door. "Can I just talk to you for a minute?"

"What's going on?"

"Shhhhhh! I'm hiding!" I whispered back.

"From who?!"

"Shhhh! Those cops—are they gone?"

Her voice calmed, and softened. "I think so. Some cops came in, but they left. Why'd you think the cops were after you?"

My eyes had adjusted to the dark and I could see the confusion on Nora's face. "Can we just sit down for a minute so I can explain?"

"What? Sit down in *here*?"

"Yeah, there's a couple steps behind us."

"This is like, ah, getting pretty weird, Gerry—"

"I know, I know," I said. "Just give me a minute."

We sat down. Nora crossed her arms and frowned.

"Look," I began. "I'm in a little bit of trouble."

"Yeah. Well, I guess I figured that part out."

"You did?"

"Duh. A kid with nothing? Hiding in the woods? Now scared of police?"

"Actually, I'm in a lot of trouble, Nora. Please, if I tell you some stuff can you promise not to tell anyone?"

She lifted her shoulders as though uncertain. But what she said was "sure."

"And *please* don't turn me in."

Nora threw up her hands and glared at me. "If I was going to turn you in, don't you think I would have done that by now? I mean, why would I?"

My turn to shrug. "Why *wouldn't* you?"

For a few seconds, we sat there, her and me, not saying anything. I felt stuck. I didn't want to blow my cover and yet I realized that Nora hadn't called the cops after all. Here I was hiding though, so I had to tell her *something*.

Nora sighed. "Okay, I'll make it easy for you," she said. "When Luke and I couldn't find you, I looked at the Web page you had up on the computer. I read the story about the kid who escaped from this place called Cliffside, and now I'm putting that together with the card I found in your pants pocket and what's going on here now. So I have a pretty good idea who you are—*Michael*."

I winced, but I didn't deny it. "Yeah, well, that's me." Still, I hesitated. The truth is that I really wanted to trust Nora because not trusting anyone was lonely. Living the way I was, hiding behind a bunch of lies, took a lot of energy. Plus it was complicated—and nerve-racking, too.

I took in a breath, let it out slow, and decided to take a chance on her.

"Look, I was at that detention place called Cliffside, but I needed to get home to take care of things, so I busted out of there."

"Did you escape in a garbage truck?"

When I nodded, Nora kind of chuckled. "And is it true you hijacked a tractor-trailer truck?"

"Yeah," I told her, and I had to grin a little because no matter what, it was a pretty amazing ride.

"That's wild! How'd you know how to drive it?"

So I told her some about my dad, what he did for a living, and where I come from. But I didn't tell her the bad stuff my father did, or why I got sent to Cliffside.

"You know, I never thought you looked like a Gerry," Nora said. She sat back with her arms still crossed and scrunched up her nose. "But you don't look like a Michael either."

"That's funny 'cause no one calls me Michael," I said. "They call me Digger."

"Digger," she repeated.

I hoped I hadn't told her too much. "Been my nickname since I was a little kid. It's 'cause I called the backhoe a digger."

"Cool! I like it."

"It's better than Gerry."

"For sure! So can I call you Digger?"

I smiled a little and when our eyes met in the dim light of that closet I felt something deep inside kind of melt. "Only when no one else is around, okay? You've *gotta* keep it a secret, Nora."

"I promise," she said.

So Nora knew about me. For better or for worse.

Later, when her mother was dropping Luke and me off at the campsite, Nora whispered "Good-bye, Digger" into my ear.

———

Woody still hadn't come home. With Buddy trotting beside us, Luke and I walked down to the bathhouse to brush our teeth. After we returned to our tents, I told Luke to change and get ready for bed. When I went in to say good night I saw how he had the checkerboard all set up for a game with his dad. The board was on a small table in between their two cots. It made me feel sorry for Luke that his dad hadn't come home on time. But it also made me aware of that hole I carried around inside myself. I honestly couldn't remember my father ever playing any kind of game with me. Not checkers or Clue, Monopoly, not even cards—nothing.

"I'm sure your dad will be back by morning," I told Luke.

He didn't seem worried, but he wasn't himself either. Like he was usually full of chitchat and dumb questions. "You're not going anywhere, are you?"

"Nope," I told him. "I'll be right out there in the pup tent all night." I knew Luke was counting on me. And since the cops were keeping such a close eye on my family's home I figured I'd be hanging out here longer than I planned.

"Do you promise?" Luke asked.

"What? That I'll be here? Of course!"

But I could see he was still a little anxious so I sat down on the cot beside him. "I was thinking you ought to learn how to swim, Luke. If it's still warm out this week, maybe we can go down to the river one day and get you a lesson."

"We'll stay in the shallow part, though, right?"

"Absolutely," I assured him. "So you better get some rest 'cause it'll be quite a workout."

Luke seemed to like the idea. He took off his glasses and set them on the milk crate by his bed. Then he crawled into his sleeping bag and hugged his stuffed tiger.

I got up to leave.

"Did you know armadillos can swim?" he asked.

I turned around. "Armadillos?"

"Yeah!" Luke nodded eagerly. "An armadillo can fill itself up with air and swim across the river. I saw one do it once!"

"No armadillos around here, though, are there?" I asked him. "Don't they live in the South somewhere? Like in Texas?"

Luke ducked down and pulled the sleeping bag over his head, which I thought was a little strange. What was with him? Was he scared?

"Hey, tell you what," I said. "How 'bout if I leave Buddy in here to sleep with you tonight? Until your dad gets back."

He whipped the covers off his face. "That would be great!"

"Buddy, here!" I ordered, pointing to the rug beside Luke's cot. "Lay down." The dog did exactly as I told him. "Stay!" I ordered, showing him the palm of my hand. He didn't move. Really, for a mutt, he was an awesome dog.

I reached down to pet him on the head. "Good boy."

I felt a little tap-tap on my elbow.

"Can I ask you one more thing?" Luke wanted to know.

"Sure."

"How come Nora called you Digger?"

"What? You heard that?"

He grinned, the little devil. Then he reached a hand down to pet Buddy, and the dog licked his fingers.

I took a hard look at that kid. I felt sorry for him, sure. He seemed like a good kid. But could I trust him, too?

"All right, I'll tell you something," I said. I sat down on the edge of his cot again. "But you have to swear to keep it to yourself."

"Cross my heart, hope to die, stick a needle in my eye. What is it?"

"Gerry's not my real name."

"It's not?" His eyes tripled in size and he sat up.

"Nope. My real name's Digger. I told Nora so I'll tell you, too. When it's just you and me and Nora, you can call me Digger."

"Wow!" Luke exclaimed. "So Gerry was just your adventure name?"

I kind of laughed. "Yeah, I guess it was my adventure name." I was thinking, if only this kid knew about the adventures I'd had!

Luke was beaming like the noonday sun. "You know what?"

"No. What?"

"Luke is not my real name either. It's *my* adventure name!"

CHAPTER SEVENTEEN

AN OPPORTUNITY

"**Y**our adventure name? What do you mean?" I asked Luke.

The smile vanished from his face. "I'm not supposed to talk about it. Daddy will be mad."

He reminded me so much of Hank right then that I put both my hands on his shoulders and squeezed them. "Look at me," I said. "It's no big deal. Everybody's got secrets, right?"

Unsure, Luke nodded weakly.

"So forget it!"

But Luke didn't look convinced.

"Hey! Come on, let's read a chapter in that dog book you were reading last night with your dad."

"*Tornado*?"

"Yeah."

Luke loved this story about a dog that dropped out of the sky.

He reached into the milk crate by his bed to get the book and put his glasses back on. I didn't ask him anymore about his *adventure name*. But you can bet your boots I filed away this information.

On the second day that Woody didn't come back, I had to start thinking serious about things. My ankle and the poison ivy were better and I still wanted to get home, but not while the police were staking out my family. Besides, what if Luke's father didn't come back? Someone had to look out for the kid.

First thing I did, whenever Luke was down to the bathhouse by himself or taking Buddy for a walk, I'd rush into the tent and rifle through stuff. I was looking for money mostly, money so we could buy food, when I come across a yellow envelope in the bottom of Woody's duffel bag. Inside was the title to his truck, a couple receipts, and one other thing: a license. It was a Texas license and it had a picture of Woody that didn't look like Woody. I mean, you could tell it was him, the round cheeks, the high forehead, the foxy eyes. But in this license picture he had short brown hair and was clean shaved. The Woody I knew had longish blond hair and a full beard. And the name on the license was *not* Sherwood "Woody" Hawkins like he told me, it was Glen David Hardesty.

Huh. I wondered what that was all about.

I put the license back, covered up the envelope with clothes, and kept looking for money, but there wasn't any. Worse come to worse, I still had the three dollars in my pocket and Luke had the change from his twenty. He said it was all he had, but all together I hoped our cash would be enough for a jar of peanut butter, a loaf of bread, some milk, and a bag of ice. Other than that, Luke and me would have to survive on our own for a while.

Nora worked all weekend at the horse farm, but when she stopped by on Monday I asked if her mother could get us that food.

She frowned. "Do you have the money? She won't just buy it."

"Yeah. I think I have enough."

"It's just that every penny counts," she said. "She's trying hard to save up enough so we can get an apartment before winter."

"Sure! I understand," I said. "I wasn't asking for free food."

"But if you get desperate, tell me, okay? I could probably sneak you guys some cereal or a couple sandwiches or something."

"Thanks," I told her. But I didn't want to go begging from Nora. I was starting to really like her and I didn't want her feeling sorry for me.

"The other thing is that I'd like to look into that job at the horse farm."

She perked up. "Great! Next weekend, come with me!"

We were sitting at our picnic table after Luke and I had a supper of leftover baked beans and half each of a stale, grill-toasted burger roll. It was getting dark earlier so Luke was doing his homework under a lantern in the tent while Nora and I propped up a flashlight on a bag of napkins and started a card game.

"Where do you think Woody is?" I asked her. I was genuinely concerned, plus I hated being hungry again.

"Beats me," she said, dealing out the cards. "One time this summer he gambled all night at the casinos in Charles Town. But don't worry, he'll be back."

I picked up my cards. "Maybe we need to call him on your cell phone—"

She shook her head. "I don't have his number. Plus my cell's not charged."

Didn't she say that before?

"A couple of times my mom and I had to take care of Luke when he was late getting home," Nora went on, still arranging the cards in her hand. "He figures you're here now—and he knows you won't call the police."

All of a sudden the loud squeal of brakes and a big thump stopped our conversation. The sound was close, like maybe on the main road into camp.

A woman screamed.

Luke came running out of the tent. "What was *that*?"

Nora and I both set down our cards. I grabbed the flashlight and we three tore down the dirt road, me still favoring that ankle and doing sort of a run/hop, with Buddy right beside us. Right off, we saw a car sideways off the road in a ditch, its lights still on, and smoke pouring out of the engine. Two people stood in the road. "We're all right!" one of them called out.

Other people had gathered and were staring into the bushes. When we got close we saw the car had hit a deer, a doe it looked like, and the animal was struggling to get up.

Buddy lurched forward and started barking so Luke kneeled down and put his arms around him to hold him back. A little boy stepped toward the deer, reaching out his hand like to wanted to pet it, or help it, and I shouted a warning: "Don't! That deer is alive and those front feet can tear you to shreds!"

A woman snatched the young boy back and a couple minutes later we all watched as the deer lay down its head and took its last breath.

Nora had a hand over her mouth. There were tears in her eyes. Even Luke, still holding back Buddy, looked about ready to cry.

I glanced around at the crowd and didn't quite get it. It was too bad what happened, for sure. But while they all saw some tearful scene, I saw an opportunity—at least forty pounds of free, fresh venison. Right when I really needed it!

The man who hit the deer was on his cell phone calling for a tow truck and most of the people watching started to leave.

"Let's go," Nora said, touching my arm.

"Poor deer," Luke added. "What will happen to it?"

"The police will probably come in the morning and take it," Nora told him.

"Are you kidding me?" I asked. "No one's gonna claim it?"

"Claim the deer?" Nora asked.

"Yeah!"

"For *what*?"

"For *meat*!" I exclaimed. Every fall since I was nine years old I'd been out deer huntin' with my friend and his uncle. Brady and I, we took the hunter safety course together and my mother signed the papers so I could hunt legal. She knew how good that venison tasted! My mother cooked it about ten different ways—she *did* occasionally cook something— and it fed us for weeks.

I decided to act.

"Look," I said quietly to Nora and Luke, "will you help me?"

Nora's eyes grew big. "What do we have to do?"

"Just help me pull the deer into that little clearing," I said. "And Luke, keep ahold of Buddy and don't let him go, you hear?"

First, I approached the deer from the rear and poked it with a stick to be sure it was dead. The deer was heavy, and it took the two of us hauling together to move it to a small level clearing off the road. I handed the flashlight to Nora.

"Hold the light on the deer's belly for me, will ya?"

While Nora held the flashlight, I pulled out the jackknife, kneeled in front of the deer, and went to work. I glanced up once and caught the horrified look on Luke's face. "You might not want to watch this," I warned him.

But Nora kneeled beside me holding the light and seemed real interested as I reached deep inside the deer and groped with my hands until I found what I needed to find and cut through it with my jackknife. At that point all the organs inside the deer were freed from the body and I was able to roll everything out onto the ground.

Buddy whined and I'm sure Luke had to tighten his hold.

"Wow," Nora said. "That's the peritoneum—the thin membrane that covers all those organs. We learned it in biology." She reached out to touch it.

"I didn't know the name," I said.

"*Now* what?" Nora whispered.

"Where's the blood?" Luke piped up. "How come it doesn't smell?"

A stranger answered. "There's not much blood 'cause this here kid did one heck of a job field dressin' that deer."

We all turned to see an older guy who had been standing there watching. "Hat's off to you, boy. I used to hunt years ago and I ain't never seen anyone do as neat a job as you."

"Thanks," I said. Turning to Luke, I explained, "The only reason it would smell is if I accidentally opened the stomach. Then it would stink to high heaven."

The stranger laughed. "You're right on that!"

Luke wrinkled his nose.

After finishing, I wiped my hands off best I could on some nearby grass. Then Nora and I stood up and I cleaned the jackknife off on my pants leg. "Next thing we need to do is get this deer back up to our campsite and hang it up."

"Hang it up?" Luke asked.

"To cool off the meat and let it bleed out," I told him. I turned to Nora. "Do you know anyone has a wheelbarrow? I'm gonna need a plastic bag, too."

"*You're* going to butcher this deer?" she asked.

"Who'd you think was going to do it? Santa Claus?"

"Is deer meat good?" Luke wanted to know.

"Plenty good," I told him. "Like beef, only a little stronger. You just wait and see."

When Nora returned with what I needed, I pushed aside the deer's innards, cut out the liver, and put it in the plastic bag.

"Here," I told Luke. "Your job's to carry this back and not let Buddy get it."

Luke held it at arm's length. "What are you going to do with *that*?"

I had to laugh. "I'm gonna eat it! Fresh deer liver, are you kidding? If you're extra good, I might even let you have a piece."

"Ewwwwww!" he said. But I bet to myself that Luke would find it mighty tasty. If not, then I'd give his share to Buddy.

On the count of three, Nora and I hefted that doe into the wheelbarrow. It must've weighed a hundred twenty pounds or so. Limping, I wheeled it back to the campsite while Nora walked alongside and made sure the deer didn't fall off.

Luke pulled on my shirt. "What about all that *stuff*?" he asked. I stopped and we looked back at the shiny innards lying in the woods behind us.

"Don't worry," I told him. "The raccoons, the possums, the fox—they'll have a feast tonight. Won't be a speck of deer gut left in the morning."

Luke looked disgusted and kept glancing back at it while we walked. I had to smile, remembering the first time I watched Brady's uncle field dress a deer. Guess it's something you never forget. But I didn't find it gross, just part of life. Waste not, want not, my grandpa used to say.

Back at the campsite, I picked out a couple trees, then found myself about a four-foot-long, skinny but sturdy stick on the ground. There's a place on a deer, near a tendon on the hind leg, where you can cut a hole and run a stick through. A couple campers had stopped to watch, so once I got that stick through I asked them to help me hoist the deer up and set the ends of the stick in two different trees so the deer could hang upside down. With Nora holding a flashlight on the trees, we got the job done.

"Butt up, head down," I told Luke, "so the blood can drain out."

He seemed scared. "How much blood?"

I shrugged. "Not that much. Maybe a pint."

"What you gonna do with all that meat?" a guy asked.

"Don't have no way to freeze this meat and the weather's not cool enough to leave it hanging so tomorrow I'm gonna cut it up. Come around in the morning and spread the word," I said. "Bring a plastic bag or something to wrap up some meat."

After we had that deer hanging up high enough to be out of critter reach, I went down to the river and felt around the water's edge for a smooth, flat stone and brought it back to the campsite.

Nora had a fire going like I'd asked. The first thing I did, I put that deer liver in the big iron skillet Woody had, added a little oil, and started cooking it up. Nora had found an onion and threw slices of it in the pan, too. We had to tie Buddy inside the big tent 'cause he was barking his head off, but I figured he'd calm down in a bit. While the liver fried, I sat on one of those rickety aluminum chairs and, in the light of the fire, spit on the smooth rock I'd found and started sharpening the edges of the jackknife by rubbing the blade against the stone in a swirling motion.

"Okay. I'm like flabbergasted," Nora said, sitting in the chair beside me. "I have never seen anyone cut up a deer like that."

"It's called field dressing," I reminded her.

"Field dressing. *Amazing.* I mean, I could see all the organs, everything. It was fascinating!"

"You'd make a good hunter then," I told her.

"Or a doctor," she suggested. "You think?"

I smiled at her. "Sure! Or a doctor." I knew that was her dream.

"Really, I was impressed," she said.

When I looked over at her, she smiled at me in a way that was different, more real somehow. My face grew warm as I turned my attention back to the blade I was sharpening. Compared to the first time I met Nora, when she seemed to think I was pretty stupid, I felt like now she had some genuine respect for me.

By the time I had the knife good and sharp, the meat was done.

"Hey, Luke!" I called. "Come try some of this liver!"

But I never did get an answer from him.

———————

The next morning—when Woody *still* wasn't back—Luke and Nora had to go to school. By myself, I pushed the picnic table over by the hanging deer so I could stand on top of it to do the butchering. I tied up Buddy so he wouldn't go crazy. Then I took my sharpened jackknife and started cutting away from the legs on down, easing the hide off. As I worked, a couple people started to come around.

It wasn't long before I had the entire hide off the deer—and a small crowd watching. Somebody called out that he'd give me five dollars for the hide.

"You got it," I said. Wasn't anything else I could do with it.

I knew most of the people watching were there for a meat handout, and I was going to be good on my word. But first, I cut a few pieces of venison for not only Luke and me, but Nora and her mom, too. I wrapped the meat in a plastic bag and nestled it at the bottom of the cooler under all the ice we had left.

Standing back on the table, I went to work quartering the deer and offered up the hind quarters to several women who'd been watching me from the get-go.

"The top is real good," I told them. "Toward the bottom it'll get tough."

I handed out other chunks of venison from the shoulder area. "That's excellent for a roast," I told folks. "Don't over-cook it! If you do, you'll hate it. It'll be dry and tough. You want it just barely pink inside."

Still more people came by and asked if I had anything left

so I cut as much meat off the neck as possible and suggested it was good for stew, or making deer sausage. "Mix in a little sage, or just salt and pepper," I said.

"How about chili?" a woman asked. "Would it make good chili meat?"

"Great idea," I replied. "Barbecue, too."

It was wonderful biting into fresh venison for dinner that night. Good to have a real meal for once. And one that I provided! But let me tell you, it was a far nicer feeling giving most of that meat away.

I just hoped I wouldn't be needing more of it myself.

CHAPTER EIGHTEEN

DECEPTION

"**H**ey, how's it going?" Woody asked after slamming the door to his pickup. Like he'd never been gone for four whole days without a word. Like nothing ever happened!

I just sat at the picnic table and stared at him 'cause I was pretty ticked off that he had disappeared and left me with Luke.

He came over to the table and plopped down across from me. "Sorry," he said when he realized I wasn't going to jump up and down to welcome him home. His eyes fell away from mine. "I got in trouble and spent a couple nights in jail."

That probably explained his bloodshot eyes, the dirty hair, and rumpled clothes. But I didn't have a lick of sympathy for him.

"That's just great," I said flatly. Then I let my hands fall open. "I mean, what if I wasn't here? What would've happened to Luke?"

Honestly, it blows my mind how many adults should *not* be taking care of kids.

Woody lifted his head. "But we had a deal, you and me. I asked if I could trust you to take care of Luke when I wasn't here."

"You didn't even call us!" I shot back.

"Who was I going to call? Neither one of you has a phone!"

That sounded pretty lame to me 'cause he could have called *somebody*. I leveled my eyes at him. "You're about as good a dad as my own. And that's no compliment."

He sighed. "Where's Luke now?"

"It's Tuesday morning. He's in school."

"Good. That's good," he said. "Thanks."

I didn't say "you're welcome."

"Look, I'm really sorry," Woody said. "I love Luke more than anything else in the world. You gotta believe that. My life is nothing without that little boy—"

"Then you should've thought about him!" I suggested.

Woody nodded. "You're right. I should have. No question."

Silence for a moment. I waited for him to go on 'cause I figured he owed me an explanation.

"I'm not a perfect person," he admitted. "Not by a long shot. But God knows I do want to be a better father, even if I do have my faults."

"What is it? Drinkin'?" I asked.

He shook his head and met my hard gaze. "Not so much that as the gamblin'. I just keep thinking I'll come out ahead, that Luke and me, we'd have the extra money we need." He continued moving his head back and forth slowly. "I can't help myself. The other night I started losing big and got told

I couldn't stay at the blackjack table. I don't do too good with people telling me what to do . . . I don't know. I thought that me and Luke, getting on the road and moving to a new place, that we'd have a fresh start . . ."

He was quiet again, and again I waited. I didn't ask him to tell me his life story, but he started in anyway.

"I got in a lot of trouble when I was a boy. There was ten of us kids. We was dirt poor and I had a lousy home life with nobody caring much about me or what I did. So I skipped school a lot. I was always runnin' off, stealin' stuff. But I remember I had a guidance counselor once in high school— before I quit—and this guy told me a story about a dog trying to get away from the kite that was tied to his tail. He said no matter how far the dog run, every time he sat down to rest, he'd turn around and see the kite. He was always runnin' from it, but it was always there.

"Well, that's me all right. Was then, is now. I keep thinking a new place is a fresh start. Only I never change who I am so things stay the same."

I knew he was opening up and being truthful 'cause he wanted me to understand. And I could see that even if he did screw up, Woody loved his kid and was sorry for what he done. If anyone could understand, it ought to be me. I had a ton of faults and was plenty sorry for what I done, too, but it didn't mean I cared any less about my mom, and my brother and sister.

"Well," I said finally. I wasn't angry anymore. "You're just about out of food. There's no milk, no eggs, no cereal—

nothing." I didn't mention the venison we'd been feasting on 'cause I figured that didn't count.

"I'll make a food run right now," Woody said.

I pulled a piece of paper out of my pocket. "Here's a list I been keeping. The stuff you need most. You don't have to get the dog food. Buddy's not your problem."

Woody took the list, but he didn't even unfold or look at it. He just slid it into a pocket on the front of his shirt. "I'll take care of it right now," he said. Then he got up and left.

Somehow, we fell back into a routine that week. I kept a low profile at the campsite but even so, I had a lot of new friends on account of that venison. People walking by from time to time would call out, "Hey, Gerry! What's up?" and I'd wave back. Evenings, I made dinner and helped Luke with homework. But his dad was the one who come in and read to him at bedtime. Luke was still reading that book *Tornado* for school, but it's funny how no matter where they ended, Luke always wanted to start on page one. "*Tornado*, by Betsy Byars," he'd begin. "'Twister!' Pete yelled. 'Twister!'"

Mornings, I got Luke off to school, then I'd clean up and hang out until Luke got off his bus at three. After lunch one day, returning from a walk, I saw Woody's truck and caught a glimpse of him disappearing into the bathhouse with a towel over his shoulder. He must've got off work early. My eyebrows went up 'cause I'd been waiting for a chance like that.

Stepping into his tent, I looked for his jean jacket and saw it right away, tossed on his cot. He took care to hide that jacket, probably 'cause he suspected I'd go through it. Which is exactly what I did. Hurriedly, I checked out the pockets looking for the cell phone he claimed he didn't have. Found it right off, too. I quick grabbed a pencil from the crate by Luke's bed to write down the number on a candy wrapper, the only paper I could find. I needed that number in case I needed to get in touch with him in an emergency—or in case he disappeared again.

After slipping the phone back, I come across his wallet. My heart really started pounding 'cause I didn't want to get caught with *that* in my hands. Fingers shaking, I flipped through it fast. He had about ten dollars, which I didn't steal, a gas card, a credit card, and—I had to stop for a minute—his driver's license. It was a Maryland license and this time the picture looked just like the Woody I knew with blond hair and a full beard. But the name was not the same as the one on the Texas license. This license had the name Sherwood Hawkins. And I wondered: was that Woody's *adventure name*?

One of those licenses was a fake. I knew it was an important discovery. Woody was hiding something. *But what?* I stuffed everything back in the wallet, shoved it into the pocket where I found it, then got myself outside fast.

Taking a deep breath to calm myself, I decided I wouldn't say anything. After all, I was using a phony name, too. Woody wasn't coming after me, so I wouldn't go after him. Not unless I had to. But it bothered me, this little secret. It was one thing for Woody to make up stuff about himself, but he had a little kid to take care of. Something was up, and I knew none of it could be good for Luke.

On Saturday morning of that week, Woody fried up some sausages and made us blueberry pancakes. A real treat. Then he and Luke left for the nearby city of Frederick to buy Luke some new sneakers and catch a movie. I washed the dishes and went to the horse farm to see about getting work. I rode over to the farm with Nora and her mom and guessed that the farm was about a mile from the campground. If I got hired, I thought, I could walk over, but I'd have to find a way to get there without being seen from the road.

"Heavenly Days?" I asked from the backseat, reading the mailbox sign.

"It's a horse rescue facility," Nora said. She looked at her mother, sitting beside her up front. "Can you explain it, Mom?"

"Yeah, sure. All the horses at this farm are here because the authorities—the courts in Maryland—took them away from abusive owners. Mrs. Crawford, who runs the place, rehabilitates them and then tries to find homes for them."

"Like foster care for horses," I said.

"Exactly!" Nora smiled at me, and I was thinking she looked especially cute the way she had braided her hair.

Nora's mother looked at me in the rearview mirror. "You're not afraid of horses then?"

"No way," I told her. "I'm not afraid of anything."

I got introduced right off to the farm owner. Mrs. Crawford was a short woman in blue jeans, boots, and an oversize flannel shirt. She pulled her thick gray hair back into a ponytail and had a face with a lot of wrinkles, but I had absolutely no idea how old she was. Could've been forty, fifty—even sixty.

"Nora says I can trust you," Mrs. Crawford said. "You a hard worker?"

"Sure thing," I answered.

"You're hired then. I'll pay you cash on Friday," she said. And the best part? She didn't make me fill out any forms or show an ID.

"Can you show him around?" Mrs. Crawford asked Nora. "Then teach him how to punch in on the time clock and get started on those stalls?"

Nora gave me a little tour, and I could tell right off this farm was a place she loved. She pointed out two herds of horses in two separate fields. "Geldings are in one pasture, the mares are in the other," she said. "A really beautiful stallion is in the barn along with horses that need the most care." That meant the horses who came in starving or sick, and had their ribs showing and chunks of hair falling out.

Horses weren't the only animals at the farm. Nora curled her slender arms around the necks of two miniature donkeys named Winston and Earl to give them hugs (I couldn't help but be a little jealous) and introduced me to three goats who tried to nibble at my hands.

Most of the farm buildings were run-down, but the

volunteers at the farm had a nice, air-conditioned room with a couch to sit on, and—I couldn't help but notice—all kinds of snacks on the table. All these places, I thought, I'd check 'em out good later on 'cause I was still on the hunt for something I could use for a weapon, if only to protect myself from my father when I got home.

A couple Mexican guys, Hector and Miguel, also worked at the farm. "They're illegals," Nora whispered as we watched them carry buckets of feed. She said they didn't speak much English, but it wasn't like I wanted to strike up a conversation with them anyway. Even though I had Spanish in middle school no way could I understand 'cause they spoke too fast. Nora introduced us—*en español*—but when those guys rattled off something in Spanish and laughed, I figured it was an insult. Was it my poison ivy? I narrowed my eyes and balled up my fists.

"Gerry! Hector! Miguel!" Mrs. Crawford called out. "I need you boys to unload this hay and stack it in the loft above the stalls."

I hopped up onto the back of the truck and started grabbing hay bales, but right away I saw that the hay was damp, like it hadn't dried out before getting cut. My grandfather never would have stacked it. He'd dry it out first. "It's wet!" I called out to Mrs. Crawford. "You sure you want to stack it?"

Miguel and Hector laughed and looked at me funny. What? Did they think I was just saying that 'cause I was lazy?

Mrs. Crawford returned to the truck. "I know. But I can't afford to wait," she said. "Let's just get it all in the barn. Maybe I can move it around later."

When we finished with the hay, Nora showed me the wild stallion in the barn. He was a pretty horse, kind of reddish brown with a long, gold-colored, but snarled, mane, and hair that fell over his eyes. When he spotted us looking at him, he laid his ears flat, turned around, and kicked the wall where we were standing.

We jumped back. "Best to stay away from him," Nora warned. I liked it when she put her hand on my arm. "There's a lot of hostility bottled up in him. He already bit Miguel once."

"What's he so mad about?" I asked.

"His previous owner kept him nailed into his stall. He never went outside, wasn't fed regular, and his stall never got cleaned out. When he was rescued, he was walking on three feet of his own manure packed down. His head almost brushed the ceiling! Honestly, we thought he'd never put his head up again. Guess you can't blame him for hating people. Miguel started calling him Fuego (she pronounced it *f-way-go*) and the name stuck. It means fire in Spanish."

After Nora showed me how to punch in on an old-fashioned time clock, I got down to business mucking out those stalls. This meant shoveling manure into a wheelbarrow, which I pushed behind the barn and dumped into a big pile. After a stall got cleaned out, I shook straw over the floor. In no time, sweat was dripping down my face and my back. All afternoon, while I worked, I heard Fuego snort and kick the wall whenever anyone passed by. He sure was ticked off at the world, I thought.

I had a lot of time to think while shoveling that manure. I thought about all the food I could buy (if I had to) with the money I was earning. I thought about Nora—how could I not? I thought about how Hector and Miguel had already gotten under my skin. I even thought about some of the things Woody had said. Like how I was either running *from* something, or *to* something. And the dog that had the kite tied to his tail. I thought about Fuego, too, this horse named for fire, who had been nailed into his stall and sometimes not fed for days. It's no wonder he didn't trust nobody and kept kicking at the wall.

In some ways, I finally realized, even if he was an animal, that horse was a lot like me.

The following week, while Luke was in school, I worked at the farm every day mucking stalls. *Mucking*—that sure was the perfect word. It was boring, back-breaking labor. Buddy and I made our way to and from the farm by walking behind a little shopping center, then paralleling the road about a hundred feet away, just inside the tree line. At one road intersection where there was a good bit of traffic, I crouched and made my way through a water culvert under the road.

When I got to the farm, I filled a bucket with water for Buddy and told him to lie down in a shady corner to wait for me. "No barking," I said, and darned if that dog didn't just lay there quiet for hours waiting for me. Well, except for the first day when he took off after the goats. And then that one time he saw the gray barn cat.

Every day, I checked out a corner of the farm by opening grain bins, pulling out drawers, and poking around in barrels and boxes. Like I said, I didn't know what I was looking for, but something would spark an idea, I was sure of it. Always, I tried to stay out of sight. One afternoon, when some state inspector guy came to check the barn, I scooted into a field and pretended to be scrubbing the water troughs.

I worried a little that Miguel and Hector might be watching me. Neither ever spoke to me but they hid behind their Spanish and seemed amused whenever I got close. I was tempted to straighten them both out with my fist, but I didn't want to lose the job. Ha! Mr. R. would've been proud of me for using the ole if/then thinking. *If I punched them out, then I'd probably get fired.* So, for the most part, I ignored those guys, except for the day I caught Miguel smoking.

What happened is I was taking a bucket of manure out back to the pile. If I'd had the wheelbarrow Miguel would've heard me coming. I just had that bucket though and I caught him red-handed, lighting up a cigarette behind the barn. There was no smoking allowed at the farm and everyone knew it 'cause Mrs. Crawford had about a million signs up. She was paying us so I figured we ought to respect that. When Miguel saw me he took the cigarette out of his mouth and dropped his hand to his side quick, trying to hide it.

I threw manure on the pile and stood there, holding the bucket and staring at him. "Mrs. Crawford said no smoking," I told him, pointing to his hand. *"No fumar,"* I added, surprising the hell out of him that I knew any Spanish at all.

He tossed the cigarette on the ground and snuffed it out with his shoe. Then he flashed his dark eyes at me. He looked a lot like Tio then. I couldn't help myself; I smiled at him.

On Friday of that week I got paid—get this—$130.50 for eighteen hours of work. I got it in two fifties, one twenty, one ten, and two quarters. It was more cash than I ever held in my hands at one time. Mrs. Crawford had told me it was cash "under the table," which meant she wasn't taking any taxes out of it. I told her "thanks," but she seemed embarrassed and asked me not to talk about it. She didn't tell me it was illegal. I found that out from Nora.

"My mom is paid under the table, too," she said. "Then she goes into town and collects unemployment."

"That's good!" I said.

But Nora shook her head. "No, it's not. She's scamming the government. I mean I'm glad she gets money so we can eat. But it's wrong."

"Why?"

Nora dropped open her mouth like, duh, you stupid bonehead. "Because if like no one paid taxes there wouldn't be money for libraries, hospitals, schools, ambulances, police—"

"Fine with me if no police!" I stopped her.

She waved me off. "Just because you're in trouble right now you think that. But if we didn't have police and courts and stuff, this world would be chaos!"

I didn't debate her anymore after that. I decided Nora thought too much about things, and I didn't know if that was good or bad. But she did make me wonder about all the deception. Mrs. Crawford did a great thing saving horses, but here she was cheating the government. And wasn't I deceiving everybody with my fake name? And Woody with his? And Hector and Miguel 'cause they snuck into this country? Not to mention my deadbeat father who sobered up and apologized and got out of trouble nearly every time my mother called for help . . . My heart skipped a beat 'cause who did she call when my father got out of control? *The police.*

I frowned. Maybe, I thought, all this deception was how the world operated. I wasn't sure. But that pile of money in my hand was real and I figured that's what counted. It was hard-earned and it would help me get home. I felt squirmy coming to this conclusion, but I was glad the government wasn't getting a chunk of it.

CHAPTER NINETEEN

BAD CHOICES

"**D**igger!" Nora called my name as she sprinted down the main road into camp, her long hair flying out behind her.

What? Was she eager to see me? I was just returning from work at the farm, that's all. But maybe we had something going, her and me. I felt the corners of my mouth start to lift.

"Digger, they're looking for you!" Nora exclaimed as she practically plowed into me. I caught one of her arms while she put the other on her chest and tried to catch her breath. "They're asking if anyone has seen this teenager—this teenager, Michael Griswald—who goes by the nickname Digger!"

"Whoa."

"You need to hide!"

"Where?"

"This way!" she said, pulling me into the woods.

We took off together, jumping over logs, dodging branches, and pushing aside the prickly underbrush. When we got to the towpath, we paused to look both ways quickly—we were breathing hard—then darted across the path and followed a narrow, winding trail to the river. Buddy was close behind us the whole way.

Nora stopped me. "See those rocks?" she asked, pointing out over the water.

"Yeah, sure." A whole series of big, white boulders dotted the river at this point. Dark water churned around and between them as it rushed downstream.

"They'll take you clear across the river. Most of the rocks are pretty flat so you can practically walk all the way across. Hide on the other side and when the coast is clear I'll go get you."

"What about Luke?" I asked.

"I'll get him at the bus and tell him not to say anything. Go on! Go *now!*"

"Come on, Buddy!" I said, slapping my leg so he'd follow. Turning, I stepped on a rock close to shore, then the next one, and the next, picking my way across the river in just a few minutes. I only needed to jump once, but I made sure to land on my good ankle.

When I got to the other side, I hid behind some bushes. Buddy sniffed around for a while, then settled down and curled up for a nap. Meanwhile, I waited for what seemed like forever. I counted last week's pay, which I'd kept in my pocket, about ten times, ate two granola bars I took from the volunteers' room, and listened to two different trains go by on the opposite side of the river. But mostly, I just sat there, peeking through the bushes, cleaning my fingernails with my jackknife, and watching for Nora. I worried about what would happen, but it felt nice that Nora wanted to protect me.

Just before it started to get dark, I spotted her. She looked like a ballet dancer the way she held her arms out and hopped, real delicate like, from one rock to the next. I went to meet her and reached out to help her onto shore. She took my hand and it was kind of nice that she didn't let go right away.

"What's happening?" I asked.

"Police are still there," she said, reaching down to pet Buddy, who was pretty excited to see her, too. "But they parked on down the road. Maybe they're waiting for you to show up. I'm sure some people at the campground figured it was you, but I don't think anyone's said anything."

"Is Luke okay?"

"He's fine. He's doing his homework. Woody should be home soon, but I'm sure *he* won't say anything. He needs you here for Luke."

I almost laughed. "Yeah."

Nora and I sat on the ground behind the bushes. I let out a long sigh. "Looks like I get to sleep in the woods again."

"You don't have to," Nora said.

"What do you mean?"

"You can go back to the horse farm and sleep in the volunteers' room."

"Really?" I was surprised. "You think it would be okay?"

"I don't think so. I *know* so." She paused a second. "My mom and I lived in that room for six months."

"*Six months?* Are you kidding?"

"I wish I *was* kidding," she said. "We had to stay there. Mom didn't have any money. I mean, we have the tent now, but we didn't have it then. Even if we did, we wouldn't have had the money to pay the campground fee. Mrs. Crawford was incredible. She didn't care if we slept there, just so long as we picked up before the volunteers arrived. Mom slept on the couch, I slept on the floor. We kept our stuff in the car."

I looked at her, kind of dumbfounded. It was hard for me to believe she actually lived in the volunteers' room for half a year. I mean, I could see myself doing that, but not her. She didn't look like a homeless person.

"Wow," is all I said.

"Yeah. *Wow* is right. My mom sometimes makes bad choices when it comes to boyfriends. I mean I know she's lonely, but still. This boyfriend she has now? He's married!"

"He is?"

Nora nodded. "He's stupid, too." She picked up a stick next to her and broke it into two pieces. "He actually makes fun of me when I try to do my homework. Which is why I'm always hanging out with you and Luke."

My heart dropped a little. "Hey, I thought you come over to be with me!"

"I do! Oh, I mean I like being with you guys, too."

I waited for her to say more. Waited while she used the sharp end of one of the sticks to draw a circle in the sand. It was a warm night and Nora wore a sleeveless top. In the soft light of dusk I watched the rose tattoo on her shoulder move with the motion of her arm.

"I'll tell you this," she said. "I am not living the way my mother lives. I want to get a scholarship and go to college.

If I can't afford medical school, then maybe I'll be a teacher, or a physical therapist. For sure, I'm going to make enough money to live in my own place."

We sat quiet for another minute—sometimes I just did not know what to say—while she made loops around the circle in the sand, turning it into a daisy. I felt anxious 'cause I really liked Nora. I even wondered if she could be like a girlfriend. I'd never had a girlfriend before. What girl would want a boyfriend who lived in a junky house without a toilet and who sometimes wore the same shirt to school for a week 'cause his mother didn't have change for the Laundromat?

"What about you?" she asked. "How come you're running away from that juvenile prison place?"

Did I want to tell her more than she already knew? I hesitated and watched her draw a stem and leaves on the dirt flower.

"You never told me, but what did you do to land yourself in prison?"

When I didn't answer, Nora stopped drawing. She tilted her head as she peered over at me and arched her eyebrows. "You didn't kill anybody, did you?"

Could she see the blood drain out of my face?

I couldn't help it. Tears sprang into my eyes. It had been such a long time since I felt myself cry that I touched my face to see if it was really happening. Embarrassed, I turned away from Nora, hoping she couldn't see.

She dropped the stick and put a hand on my shoulder. "Digger?"

I sniffed.

"Are you crying because I asked about what you did? Look, you don't have to talk about it if you don't want to. It's just me, dumb ole Nora asking stupid questions." She put her entire arm around my shoulders.

"It's complicated," I mumbled.

And that was the truth. A lot of stuff about me was complicated and some of it for reasons I didn't even understand. But this I knew: there was a ton of heavy guilt for what I done to end the life of three-year-old Benjamin DiAngelo. Even if I didn't mean to hurt that little boy, I did. I took his life away from him and it left me with a heaviness that I carried around with me, day and night, like a solid iron brick. I tried not to think about it, but it was always there, every day, everywhere I went. When I got up in the morning, when I sat down to eat, when I lay down to sleep, when I squatted in the woods—and especially, when I looked up at the night sky.

Like I said before, I didn't have religion like J.T. and Abdul. That was something for normal kids in regular families that eat dinner together and take vacations and go to the mall for school clothes. But there were times looking up at those stars at night that I wished deep in my heart that there really was something spiritual, some everlasting life somewhere so that little Ben lived on.

"Maybe it would help if you talked about it," Nora urged gently.

I nodded and my throat got tight. She was probably right. It would probably help me to talk about it. But I wasn't the type to talk about stuff. Miss Laurie had to work for days to drag a couple things out of me. It didn't mean I wasn't suffering though. I suffered plenty whenever I thought about Ben and what I done. And not only that, but I thought about what I lost because of it. When I sabotaged the red kayak and Ben died, I also lost my two best friends. And the cold, hard truth is that I didn't think I could ever get them back. Not even in ten years.

"Digger?"

I felt tears run down my cheeks.

"Hey, come on, Dig, are you okay?"

I had a hand over my eyes, but I used it to wipe the tears off.

"Really, you don't have to say anything," Nora insisted.

But I guess I *did* want to say something because the words finally rose up and came out of my mouth. "I've made some unbelievably bad choices in my life, too," I said.

Then, bit by bit, I ended up telling Nora the whole story of what I done. I described how I had drilled holes in a red kayak to make it sink so I could get back at my snooty neighbor. How I forced my friend J.T. to help me by standing guard, which is why he got sent away to prison, too. And sadly, how I had no idea my neighbor's wife and their little boy would be the ones to take that boat out for a ride one morning in early April, not knowing it would spring a leak and sink.

"The Chesapeake Bay is still really cold in April," I had to explain to Nora. "After the kayak took on water . . . a little kid . . . water in his lungs . . . they tried to save him but it was too late . . ."

Then I told her how my other best friend Brady found out what I done. And how I begged him not to tell, but how he went to the police anyway, which was really the right thing to do. I also told Nora how I stood up in court and insisted to everyone it wasn't J.T.'s fault and how nobody should hold anything against Brady either, even if he did plant the idea in my head a long time ago.

"Nine months at the juvenile jail place was the punishment. So that's it. That's what I done. That's why I'm supposed to be at Cliffside."

There was a long pause after I finished talking. Nora was stone quiet. I snuck a glance at her. She had taken her arm away, but wasn't drawing in the dirt anymore. She was just sitting there, hugging her knees.

"I don't get it," she finally said. "I mean, it's so awful what happened, and you're so sorry. Why aren't you out there serving time for what you did?"

A good question. An excellent question! Nora was right. She was right, too, about the world needing police and courts and all that. I knew I should be serving my time. Absolutely. Let justice be done!

I shifted position and turned slightly away from her because I didn't want to have to tell her about my mother and my brother and sister. How I needed to protect them from my father. Those things were important, too, but it seemed like that was offering up a layer way too deep, and way too personal.

"I got my reasons," I told her.

"I hope they're good ones, Digger," Nora replied. "Because, like what gives you the right to take the law into your own hands?"

"What do you mean?" I heard my voice get loud and felt my right hand automatically form a fist.

Nora didn't seem to notice the anger. "When you ran away from that juvenile detention center, you broke the law. Maybe you had a reason, but still, you broke the law. You did it again when you stole that big truck—"

I wheeled all the way around to face her. "You thought that was pretty cool, me stealing that truck!"

She nodded, but she looked pained. "Yeah, I did, I know. But that doesn't make it right."

Nora was pissing me off with her questions. She didn't understand why I busted out and ran away. I *had* to run. I had to run to survive! I needed to get home and fix things!

But which was it? Survive? Fix things? Fix things *how*?

The questions made my head hurt. I didn't have the answers. What's done was done, I decided. I wasn't sorry I broke out of prison. I wasn't sorry I stole that truck—*or* that bike—*or* that canoe! To hell with those people! All of them had far more stuff than I would ever have! As for my father . . . he would get what he deserved someday. Every time I thought about him it made my blood boil.

I got up, confused—and angry.

"Digger?"

"I got my reasons!" I yelled at her. Then I stormed away.

CHAPTER TWENTY

TRUE HAPPINESS

By the end of October a lot of little things started to change. The days got cooler and nights downright cold. I needed an extra blanket when I slept and had to start wearing that dang Redskins sweatshirt all the time, even when we sat around the fire after dinner. Other things happened, too, things I never noticed before I lived in a tent. Like all the acorns that thumped on the roof and how the crickets got loud and how geese flew overhead making long, wavering checkmarks in the sky. In the mornings, there was dew on the grass. It was dark when Luke left for school. And, as Nora liked to point out, the poison ivy leaves had turned red.

I couldn't stay mad at Nora for long. I told her I was sorry for stomping off and she said not to worry about it. But after that, she didn't ask me any more questions about my past, or why I run away from prison, and I didn't ask her anything about her personal life. We both had screwed-up families and lives. In a weird way, it gave us a bond.

Anyway, the little changes at the end of October hinted

that bigger changes—like winter—were on the way. Some people at the campground had already left for the South to pick oranges. Nora, upset one night, said her mom was thinking of moving to Las Vegas with her boyfriend. Even Woody mentioned something about working on bridge construction in Florida. I knew I'd have to make a big decision of my own pretty soon. All of which was unsettling. So I played a lot of basketball to get my mind off stuff.

Thump, thump, thump—clang! Thump, thump, thump, whoosh!

I loved the sound of a basketball swishing through the rim, all net. Ever since my ankle had healed up Luke and me had been regulars on the campground court, practicing foul shots and layups with the basketball Woody bought.

"Luke, stop! If you're coming toward me and I'm defending the basket, then switch the ball over to your other hand. Keep your body between me and the ball!"

"Got it!" he hollered back, but he had a hard enough time dribbling with his right hand, much less his left.

Nora got in on some of the basketball, too, and I have to say, she was a pretty good shooter. I felt bad she might be moving to Las Vegas, but I didn't say anything, and I tried not to think about it.

A month had passed since I ran away from Cliffside. A whole week since I hid from police across the river. Buddy and I spent that night sleeping in the volunteers' room at the horse farm, like Nora suggested, and it wasn't that bad. I had a couch to sleep on, a bathroom, and a bunch of snacks. Nora took care of Luke for me until Woody got home that night, and Buddy and I were back in the morning before Luke had to go to school so it wasn't ever a problem.

I continued working at the farm a lot and one day, I offered to build some shelves for Mrs. Crawford in the tack room where they keep all the bridles and saddles. She had a couple nice pieces of pine and a table saw in a toolshed. She said her husband was going to make her some shelves about five years ago, but then he up and had a heart attack and died on her. Funny—not about him dying—but the fact that I actually learned in wood shop at the prison how to cut, plane, and build wooden shelves. Before I took off, us boys in shop made a slew of shelves for New Germany State Park.

While I was in the toolshed working, I hid both a hammer and a hacksaw. But the next day I put them back on the wall over the bench 'cause I could get a hammer at home. And a hacksaw was just too big and clumsy to carry. Besides that, realistically, how the heck was I going to use a hacksaw for protection?

Anyway, after the shelves got done, Mrs. Crawford started giving me more hours of work and different jobs. Like one day she asked me to put fly spray on the horses. She also taught me how to turn my back to a horse, lift its foot, and clean out under the hoof with a pick. Bet you didn't know stuff could rot under there. That not only smelled bad, but could cause a painful crack in the hoof, too.

One weekend, I even sat in on a session with Nora and the volunteers to hear a talk about emergency situations. Like if a horse got loose or the barn caught fire or—and this is wild—if some crazy horse owner showed up at the farm wanting to steal back the horse that had been taken away. We learned how to size people up quickly. Do they look you in the eye? Are they impatient? Do they keep asking about a particular horse and want to see it?

I loved being at the farm with Nora on the weekends. She was happy around those horses and knew all their names, their personalities, everything. Like how you couldn't put Mozart next to Prince. And how Pegasus had to be the first one in the gate to eat. And how Tork stood at the rail and chewed on the wood, which is called cribbing, which is a bad habit like biting your nails, only worse.

She had a soft spot for that crazy stallion, Fuego, and even brought out handfuls of Cinnamon Cheerios from the volunteers' room and left them on his paddock door for a treat. She talked sweet to him and one day—it blew me away— I saw that horse come over and let her pet his nose. "It's like velvet," she said softly. "Here, come touch it. Go ahead. Isn't it amazing?"

Nora taught me a lot about horses. Like the hair that hung over Fuego's eyes? That was his forelock. I watched Nora straighten out his forelock so he could see. Then she gave him a good hard scratch under that forelock and it must've felt good 'cause he closed his eyes.

So the farm was working out, but I still hadn't found anything that would make a good weapon or give me any idea of how I was going to protect my mom and the kids. And that was beginning to worry me.

Meanwhile, I was making money, most of which I saved. The only money I spent was for dog food. Plus I gave Woody some cash one time to buy me a couple plastic razors. My dad had grown a beard recently and I didn't want to start looking anything like him. So I had almost five hundred dollars saved up and stuffed into a sock with the white card from Cliffside. I kept the sock deep inside my pillowcase in the pup tent.

At the campsite, things were pretty good, too.

One evening after dinner, me, Luke, Woody, and Nora took this rusty, paint-chipped set of silver and gold horseshoes Woody had and walked down to the playground where they had two sandy pits staked out under the trees.

"I want Nora!" Luke cried out. And I thought, darn, 'cause I wanted Nora, too. She was looking mighty cute with her hair in braids and a snug black T-shirt she'd worn once before that said: I DID THE MATH: HORSES > BOYS. Which made me wonder all over again if she felt that way.

Luke's a little kid so we all shrugged and let him have his way and paired off. We even let Nora and Luke go first.

"Do you need glasses?" I asked Nora when her horseshoe missed the stake by about five feet.

She slapped me on the arm and then watched me throw a perfect ringer.

Luke was next and his throw was terrible. It didn't land anywhere near the pit.

"Try again," I heard Woody tell him. "That was your practice shot."

But Luke's second try wasn't any better, and I could see this game was going to be a slaughter. Nora was taking it in good humor, shrugging like who cares? But Luke was already getting pouty and sad.

My partner, Woody, was next. But before he took his turn, he caught my eye and kind of nodded before sending his horseshoe a whopping twelve feet off the mark.

Now, it's not my nature to let somebody else win if I can help it, no way, but I could tell Woody wanted me to play along. He was doing it so Luke and Nora would win, so Luke wouldn't feel bad. I understood all that, but I also thought it was kind of teaching Luke to be a crybaby so he'd get his way.

"Go ahead! Aim careful there, boy!" Woody called out when it was my turn again.

I held the horseshoe in front of my face and squinted my eyes as I took aim.

"Whoa!" I hollered when my horseshoe overshot the pit and landed in the bushes.

Luke laughed. "What happened to *you?*"

So basically me and Woody, we let them win. Luke went running to his dad, who picked him up high in the air and gave him a big hug.

And you know what? It didn't bother me a lick that I gave in 'cause it was so nice, seeing that kid and his dad look so happy.

Nights, I was sharing Buddy with Luke. Like one night the dog would sleep in the big tent, and one night he'd sleep with me. I didn't care too much about it. I worked hard and was tired at night. No television in the pup tent, but Woody did give me an old radio and a couple times I turned it on. I couldn't find a Ravens game, so I listened to music and some of the World Series games.

Funny, but I didn't even miss TV, and it had always been like this really big part of my life. Back home, even though we didn't have a flush toilet in our house, we had three televisions. I watched cartoons like *SpongeBob* and *Dora* with Hank and LeeAnn and then all kinds of crazy stuff at night. My parents didn't care. Even at prison, us boys could watch television. If you didn't have kitchen duty, you could go to the "40-scater," this big room off the dining hall where a TV was rigged up to a satellite box. No cable television out there in the boonies! Problem with the satellite setup though was that the control box was in the office so we couldn't change the station. They kept it on ESPN for sports, so that's all we saw: football, basketball, baseball, golf, poker, whatever was on. Sometimes, we got to see a movie, but nothing ever R-rated. Other than *The Mummy* all those boys ever wanted to see was more sports. I think if I had to watch *Remember the Titans* or *Hoosiers* one more time I would've puked.

Without TV, I had a lot of "think time" in that tent. Funny how when you're by yourself and it's quiet, you see things more clearly. For example, while listening to Luke and his dad read that dog story every night I noticed how Luke always started with Chapter One. Then, at some point, he'd push the book to his father and say it was his turn. And it just kind of struck me all at once—was Luke trying to memorize the story? Like maybe he *couldn't* read! Maybe memorizing the story was how he faked it!

I sat up when that thought hit me. It sure would explain why every time I helped him read, we did the same sentence over and over before moving forward. Huh. So what was up with that?

Lots of times I thought about Nora and how much I liked her. I knew it was one reason I wasn't rushing off. And sometimes, I got to thinking about all those things Nora asked me. Like what gave me the right to take off from Cliffside and steal that truck? I kept coming to the conclusion that she didn't understand my mission. Sometimes, I thought, I should forget Nora and everyone else, just drop everything and get on home to help Mom. If things were bad, if I got desperate for protection, I could steal this rifle my neighbor kept behind the vacuum cleaner inside his broom closet. My neighbor didn't know I watched him put his gun away one evening while I was returning a casserole dish to his wife. He'd been trying to kill the fox that cruised our neighborhood 'cause they had a Chihuahua or something like that, one of those little dogs that would make a nice snack for a hungry red fox.

But those neighbors with the rifle? They brought my mom a bag of groceries once. They made us dinner when my mom got sick. Another time they paid our electric when it got turned off. The white card flashed in my mind: *Think of the other person.* How could I break into their house after all they done for us?

Besides, wasn't I kidding myself to think I could get away with a prank like that? Stealing a rifle? Then actually *using* it? The white card again: *If I stole a rifle, then I'd probably get caught and spend even more time in prison!* I'd never get to be a Marine. I wouldn't be able to see Hank and LeeAnn grow up. I wouldn't have a life, period. And would it really make things better? Or was I doomed to making everything worse?

Damn that white card. It made me think too much! I pulled it out from inside my pillowcase and got ready to tear it in half. But then I flipped it over 'cause for some reason I'd been trying to remember the last "expectation" on the back side. Number twelve. Oh, yeah. "I will actively involve myself in planning for the future and in developing my aftercare plan." I started to smile. Mr. R. and Miss Laurie, for sure they wouldn't think my future plans right now were very good! No . . . I felt the smile kind of slide off my face . . . they wouldn't. They'd be ashamed.

Then it happened again.

"Woody's gone," I told Nora. "He never came home last night."

She rolled her eyes and dropped her backpack on the picnic table. It was Saturday and Nora and I didn't have to work until later. The three of us were headed to the river with a blanket, a deck of cards, and a picnic lunch. But I had Woody's cell phone number with me, too. It was written on the candy wrapper that I'd pushed into my pocket. At the very least, I'd call Woody and chew him out for leaving us again. Then I might call Mom, just to see how she was doing.

So we were down at the river. It was a pretty day. People called it Indian summer on account of how it stayed warm so late into November. Nora had already ditched her backpack so she and Luke could go off looking for sea glass along the shore. That left me alone. I knew Nora would tell me her phone wasn't charged up. I didn't know why she didn't want me using it. While she was gone I took a breath, then hastily rummaged through her backpack. I pushed aside her *Vocabulary for the College-Bound Student* book and her Shakespeare paperback and all her notebooks with a million roses doodled all over them until I found the little, silver flip-top cell phone. I checked to be sure she wasn't coming, then I flicked that cell open—and just stared at it. There wasn't even a number pad. It was a broken, empty shell.

Without skipping a beat, I snapped the phone shut, dropped it deep in the backpack, and rearranged the books. I didn't need to ask Nora about that busted-up phone. I knew why she carried it around. She probably even had pretend conversations on it at school. I knew how she felt. Middle school was bad enough. I couldn't imagine high school.

Suddenly, Nora was there. "What's wrong?" she asked.

"Nothing," I said, taking in a big breath. Boy, she picked up fast on a mood.

She had a handful of colored glass that she was going to turn into jewelry. "You remind me of a joke," she said, sitting on a rock. "What did the bartender say when a horse walked into the bar?"

I smiled, shook my head, and shrugged. "No idea. What?"

"Why the long face?"

I laughed. But I didn't know any jokes. "Don't nod," I told her.

"What?"

"Don't nod. It's a palindrome. The same thing forward and backward."

I could almost see the wheels turning in her brain. She pressed her lips together, thinking. "I have one! Fall leaves after leaves fall."

I frowned. "That's not a palindrome."

"It *is*!" Nora insisted. "Not by letters, but by words."

"It doesn't count then."

Nora scowled and set down the sea glass. When she looked skyward, thinking, the silver stud in her nose sparkled and her long shiny hair fell back loose over her shoulders. She sure was different, I thought, and she sure was pretty.

Suddenly, she caught my eyes and just held them. I stared back until she leaned forward, elbows on her knees and face in her hands. "You know what?"

"What?" I asked.

"You're really cute."

I snorted and dropped my eyes.

"No. Really. You are, Dig. I couldn't tell before because of all the poison ivy. But now that it's gone, I can see. Even that little chip in your tooth is cute."

I rolled my eyes. "Get out of here."

"I'm serious!"

Yikes! What do you say to a girl who's just told you you're cute?

"Actually," I began, although I knew I was going out on a limb here. "I've been meaning to tell you that you're a very pretty girl."

Man, right away I could have kicked myself it sounded so lame.

But before I knew it, she popped over to give me a kiss right on the lips! Surprised the heck out of me. I was *not* ready for that. But it sure felt nice. *Real nice.* Her lips were soft. I started to reach for her, but she jumped because suddenly Luke was coming up the path with a big chunk of purple glass, calling out, "Hey, you guys, look what I found! I'm going to put it in my rock collection!"

Five minutes later, Woody came looking for us. Not only was he back, but he had barbecue, he said, hot barbecue, rolls, coleslaw, and baked beans for a feast.

"Daddy! Daddy!" Luke shrieked happily as he ran to Woody.

"He must've made a few bucks playing blackjack," I muttered to Nora.

"Or craps," she whispered back.

"Come and get it!" Woody called to us.

Nora and I looked at each other and shrugged. "We'll have our picnic tomorrow," she said. "We'll take it over to the farm."

I don't think I've ever known what true happiness is. When people talk about finding true happiness, I'm never sure what they mean, or what it's like, never mind how they *found* it. It's true that I still had decisions to make, and things to work out in my head. But with my job at the farm, my ties to Buddy and Luke—even Woody—and the nice thing with Nora, I was getting a taste of what true happiness might be like. This is really strange, but what really took the pressure off and let me enjoy those last few days is the fact that I had died.

No kidding. I was dead.

CHAPTER TWENTY-ONE

BEING DEAD

It was Nora who told me I had died. One afternoon when I was behind the barn at the farm hosing out feed buckets, she rode her bike over. I was surprised 'cause she must've got out of school early and come straight over. "Hey!" she called out. I pretended like I was gonna hose her off, too, but she frowned and yelled, "Stop!" so I set the hose down and turned it off.

"I printed this out last night at the café—it's from news three days ago," she said, handing me a folded piece of paper.

Opening it, I read the news article she had found:

SEARCH CALLED OFF FOR DETENTION CENTER RUNAWAY

CUMBERLAND—A missing fourteen-year-old boy who ran away from the Cliffside Youth Detention Center six weeks ago is now believed to have drowned in the Potomac River. Authorities called off the search for the missing youth after discovering a stolen canoe likely used in the escape and clothing the youth was thought to be wearing. Efforts are now underway to recover the boy's body.

The search for the missing youth began in late September when the boy disappeared from the detention center. Police suspect the boy walked off the property and made his way to Route 68 where he may have stolen a tractor-trailer truck from a restaurant parking lot. The truck was later found abandoned and burning on the eastern Sideling Hill runaway truck ramp. Authorities also suspect the youth may have stolen a bicycle from campers along the C&O Canal towpath, as well as the canoe that disappeared from another campsite.

The canoe was found partially submerged in shallow water north of Harpers Ferry, West Virginia, yesterday. A sweatshirt with the name of Cliffside Youth Center was found upstream on the opposite shore, and a hat possibly taken from the owner of the stolen truck was found floating near Dam No. 5.

I folded the article back up and slowly pushed it into my pants pocket. When I got back to the campsite I crawled into my pup tent and slid the article inside my pillow, beside the lumpy white sock with my money and the white card. Every now and then I'd pull the paper out, unfold it, and read it again. And every time I did, my eyes misted over 'cause what it meant was that people thought I was dead.

It was an overwhelming idea. I mean, really, what did my mom think? And poor little LeeAnn and Hank? Did they cry? What about J.T.? Did he finally soften up a little when he heard I was a goner? And how about all the kids I knew from middle school? Were they sad to hear I was dead? Would they make me a memorial garden with a sundial and black-eyed Susans like they did for Allie Burdick, who got hit by a car crossing the highway in Ocean City?

Or would they say I deserved to die for what I done?

I hung my head. The police thought I had drowned, which was how most people thought Ben had died when the kayak sank. He didn't though. He was alive after he got pulled out of the river. My friend Brady brung him back to life with CPR. Only later, in the hospital, he died from aspiration pneumonia, which is what happens sometimes after people get their lungs full of water.

Whew. I covered my face with my hands. I had to stop myself from thinking about it! Reading about my death made me think of Ben all over again and that was like sinking in quicksand. I mean, it was all so incredibly, horribly sad, but what was I supposed to do? Go kill myself ?

Believe me, I thought about that. But I could never kill myself. That's the ultimate cop-out. I still had a life—and I wanted to live it.

And here's the thing: if everyone thought I was dead, then they weren't looking for me anymore. The pressure was off!

I was handed a second chance on a silver platter. I could go home now without worrying about the police.

But I didn't head home right away. Because of Nora—and the fact that there was one thing I needed to do first. . . .

"You're *not* my grandfather!" Luke exclaimed.

"But I don't *have* to be!" I insisted. "That paper said if your grandparents can't make it to Grandparents Day, then you can take a special friend. Tell your teacher I'm your cousin from Texas."

Luke flashed his eyes at me. "You're not supposed to talk about Texas!"

"Oh?" I raised my eyebrows. "Why not?"

But Luke pouted and pushed away his paper plate with the grilled cheese crusts. Then he got up and went into his tent.

"All right then. Tell them I'm your cousin from Ohio!" I called after him.

No answer. It was pretty obvious he didn't want me going to school with him. But I was determined. I needed to talk to his teacher.

Two days later, I took a shower and shaved what little stubble I had. I combed my hair, which was getting kind of long, and put on my clean set of clothes—jeans and a long-sleeved dark blue T-shirt. I even wiped off my boots so I didn't track any horse manure into Harwick Elementary School.

In the hazy light of early morning, I walked with Luke to the entrance of the campground where the Number 23 bus picked up three kids. Woody had no idea what I was doing.

"It's Grandparents Day," I told the bus driver when I climbed aboard with Luke. "He doesn't have grandparents nearby so I'm kind of like his guest. I'm his cousin Gerry from Toledo."

The bus driver, a fat woman with long, gray wavy hair and greasy bangs, looked at me over her glasses and just kind of shrugged. Like she didn't care.

So Luke and me took a seat together toward the back.

"It's my cousin Gerry," Luke told a little boy who had turned around from the seat in front of us to stare at me.

"You're lucky," the boy said sadly. "I don't have anyone to bring."

"You should see him play basketball," Luke said.

The kid perked up. "Cool! Are you staying for recess?"

"Yeah!" Luke suddenly got excited. "You are, aren't you, Gerry? Can you show some of the kids how you do a layup?"

I grinned. "Sure."

A bunch of moms greeted us at Luke's school. They had a card table spread with stick-on labels and felt-tip pens. "GERRY," I wrote in big black letters before slapping the label on my T-shirt.

"Welcome, Gerry!" one of the moms said. "It's really nice of you to make the effort to be here today."

I think Luke was changing his mind about me going to school with him. He reached up and took my hand and led me down the hallway to his room. On the way, he pointed up on the wall to show me the turkey he had drawn using his hand as a pattern. All the other turkeys taped to the wall had little poems underneath.

"Where's your poem?" I asked Luke.

"I didn't have time to finish," he said.

Exactly, I thought to myself. He can't read so he can't write either. I had asked him about all this a couple nights ago.

"Yes," he had insisted. "Of course I can read."

"Then read me the last chapter of *Tornado*," I challenged him.

"No." He crossed his arms. "I don't have to."

"No. But you and me, we both know you can't read."

Luke pouted and stared at the floor.

"Don't do you no good to pretend you're somebody you aren't," I told him. "It'll catch up to you someday and by then, maybe, it'll be too late."

Wow. Had I really said that to him? Me? The great pretender?

"Come on, dude," I said. "You don't want to be late for class."

Been a long time since I was in third grade, but the room looked and felt familiar to me with the little desks, the sound of pencils being sharpened, and the smell of those chalkboards beside the big clock on the wall.

Luke's teacher, Mrs. Buckley, had tight curly hair and wore a long yellow sweater over a flowery skirt. Her acorn earrings swung back and forth while she shook hands with us "grandparents." I waited my turn and explained again who I was. She said she was really glad that I had come all the way from Ohio. Well, I thought, we'd see about that.

Luke sat at his regular desk while I took a seat in the back with a few older people. We listened to the announcements, then we did the Pledge, and while the kids stood and sang a song about Thanksgiving, I tried to rehearse in my head what I was going to say to Mrs. Buckley. I wasn't a lick nervous about talking to that teacher. I figured she'd probably be insulted if some stranger told her one of her students was fakin' it and didn't know how to read. But I didn't care what she thought 'cause it was Luke I was trying to help. I think that's what being dead did for me. It made me fearless. Like what did I have to lose?

Recess became my opportunity. Us grandparents and special friends were told we could either go out on the playground with the kids, or stay behind for coffee and doughnuts in the teachers' lounge. Two of the people in my group went outside while the others headed for the doughnuts.

"I'll be right there," I told Luke. "Get your friends together and try to find a basketball."

Meanwhile, I kept an eye on Mrs. Buckley. When the room was empty and she was stacking papers on her desk, I approached and cleared my throat.

"Oh, my!" she exclaimed, putting a hand on her chest.

"Sorry," I said. "I didn't mean to scare you. But I wonder if I could tell you something about Luke, my little cousin, while I have the chance."

"Surely," she said, squinting at my name tag. "Have a seat, Gerry."

So I sat down in the front desk and she sat behind hers and I cleared my throat again. "I could be wrong," I said, beginning with the words I'd practiced in my head, "but I think Luke doesn't know how to read."

"Really?" Her eyebrows shot up and she folded her hands on her desk.

"Really," I said. "I think he memorizes lines and tries to fool you."

"But he did such a great job reading from *Tornado*."

"Think back, Mrs. Buckley. Did Luke read the first chapter or two? Did you hear him read from the middle or the end of that book? Like the chapter about the cat? Or the turtle maybe?"

Mrs. Buckley's brow wrinkled. "No," she said. "I don't think so. He read to us from Chapter One. I remember. He raised his hand and asked if he could start."

So we had us a talk. Mrs. Buckley promised to do some one-on-one testing and tried to explain how with thirty-five kids in the class and no teacher's aide and all the testing she couldn't give the kids the individual attention they needed. I could see Luke and about five little boys with their faces pressed up against the glass window behind Mrs. Buckley making faces. Luke had a basketball in his hands and was throwing it up and down.

"I gotta go now," I said. "Thanks for your time."

Mrs. Buckley thanked me and said again how nice it was for me to come all the way from Illinois. I ignored her little blooper and nodded, hoping she'd at least heard me right about Luke.

Boy, I hoped I did the right thing, but who knew? At least it wasn't a wasted day. I had fun with the kids at recess and us grandparents and special friends got treated to a nice lunch in the classroom. A couple moms had brought in a whole spread with chicken salad, potato rolls, chips, green Jell-O—and orange frosted cupcakes that I hoped weren't leftovers from a Halloween party 'cause Halloween was like three weeks ago.

"Dammit, I'm mad!" Nora said angrily, settling her hands on her hips.

"What do you mean you're mad? What at?"

Her scowl melted into a smile. "It's a palindrome! I finally thought of one!"

I smiled. "Ah, you got me. You're right. It is."

Friday night and it was raining cats and dogs. Woody hadn't come home yet, but I almost didn't care because Nora was there and we were all in the big tent. Luke was snuggled up with his tiger and Buddy, watching a movie on the little TV that ran on a battery. Within three days of my visit to Harwick Elementary, Mrs. Buckley had done some testing and found out Luke had a learning disability called dyslexia. He was going to get special help for it in school. At first, Luke didn't realize I did him a favor. He didn't talk to me for like six hours. But then he was back to normal.

After Nora did her palindrome, she settled into the bean-bag chair with a blanket wrapped around her 'cause it was cold. She was reading Shakespeare while I stretched out on Woody's cot beside her and closed my eyes to rest.

A few minutes went by and suddenly, Nora was at my side whispering urgently, "I can't read."

I sat up quick. "What? You, too?"

"No, not that, dummy. I mean I can't read because I'm ticked off."

"Why?"

"My mother said we're leaving next week for Las Vegas. As soon as school lets out for Thanksgiving we're gone. Just like that! So I get ripped out of school again and have to move with her and her boyfriend, who got hired at one of the casinos. Can you believe it? He's leaving his family!" Nora rolled her eyes, then she imitated her mother in a high voice: "'Oh, Las Vegas, you'll love it! It's warm year round!'"

Nora dropped her head. "It stinks. I don't want to go."

I slid onto the floor and sat cross-legged in front of Nora, then reached over to take her hands. "Boy. I don't want you to go either." I hadn't said anything to her, but I was a little bit in love with Nora. I had to be 'cause I thought about her a lot, her pretty smile, her shiny hair, her soft lips. I knew she was probably too smart for me. She'd be going off to college, but I didn't want any more school after high school. If I didn't join the Marines, then I was going to get a job driving a truck or woodworking. Something outside where I could use my hands. Maybe I wouldn't get rich doing that kind of work, but I'd be doing what I liked and I could save up, the way I had here. It being Friday, I'd added another $120 to my stash of cash and had over $700 in that sock now. Someday, I could save up again and buy a house. I'd move Mom and the kids in. It would be nice to have a steady girlfriend, too. Somebody like Nora who I could trust, like a friend. Someone who cared about me.

Gently, I pushed a loose strand of hair off her face and tucked it behind her ear. When she looked up, I saw tears in her eyes.

"Come with us!" she blurted. "Mom said you could. She said if you got a job and helped out with food you could come."

We glanced at Luke but he was into his TV show. Nora whispered, "If it doesn't work out with Mom, then you and I could run away together. We could go live with my grand-mother! She once said if I got desperate she'd send me bus money."

"What?"

"We could just take off. Sometimes, that's what I want to do. Just take off."

When she started crying I pulled the blanket up around her shoulders, wrapped my arms around her, and held her tight. Luke was faced the other way, but I hoped he didn't turn around and see.

"But why would your mother want me along?" I said softly in her ear. "And what if the cops realize I'm not dead? They'll come after all of us and you'll get in trouble, too. Really, Nora, did you think about that? Like what if they don't find a body? What did you tell me about people who drown? Their bodies always float?"

Nora pulled back and wiped the tears off her cheek. "It depends on the water temperature," she said softly, stopping to sniff. "If that river water is really cold—like you said it was—it could take a long time.

"See, Dig, what happens is that the body sinks to the bottom, right?" She had stopped whispering to explain. She couldn't help herself. She loved showing off all the stuff she knew. "It stays there until it starts to decay, then the gases from the decomposition make the body float again. But if the water is cold, if it's fresh water, then it could take longer because—"

"Okay, okay!" I put a hand up 'cause sometimes I had to stop her.

"The point is that while most bodies float in about three days, it could actually take weeks. And it's possible a body might get stuck in the rocks or something and would never surface."

"So I could stay dead for a long time?"

She nodded, then cracked a smile. "Your body might never come up!"

Perfect. I just wished that while I was dead, all the other things didn't have to change so fast. Sitting there, holding Nora's hands, I felt like for the first time in my whole entire life I didn't want things to change.

Why? Why do you suppose I felt this way? Was it because for the first time in my life I was a little bit happy? Again, I thought of how Woody had once said you're either running *from* something, or *to* something. Maybe this is what I was running *to*.

Nora opened her arms and I pulled her close again. "Okay," I murmured into her ear. She hugged me back tight.

"Okay," I repeated, "I'll go with you."

CHAPTER TWENTY-TWO

SPONTANEOUS COMBUSTION

Why not? Why not take off and go to Las Vegas with Nora? Just start over. A new life. A clean slate with somebody I loved and actually *trusted*.

I wasn't giving up on my mission. I'd just go out to Las Vegas for a few months and then make my way back. By then I'd have a better idea of what I could actually do to protect my mom and the kids.

After Nora left that night, I felt good about the decision to go with her. We'd be driving out to Nevada in her mom's car so I'd get to see the country for the first time in my life. And the great thing is that I had a nice chunk of cash to get me started. When I crawled into my pup tent that night, I started to slide my hand inside the pillowcase to count my money again only to discover that on top of the pillow was a flat sock alongside my Cliffside white card. Unfolded and spread out beneath both was the article about me being dead.

It felt like all the blood just drained out of my body I was so shocked. I knew right off who took my money: Woody. He must have come home earlier that afternoon and stole it so he could gamble. Leaving the article unfolded was his way of telling me he knew the truth about my escape.

A few seconds later, my blood was back and boiling up I was so angry. I smashed my fist into the pillow. What a lowlife scumbag, I thought. And there I was feeling *sorry* for him! Even *trusting* him! So what did that say about me? That I was a sucker? I shoved the white card and the article back in my pocket, then I balled up the sock and tossed it as hard as I could into a corner of the tent. When I saw Woody again, I'd send him flying with my fist. I'd punch him out good!

Another thing I was going to do, I was going to write a letter to Luke's teacher and tell her to have police check out the name Glen David Hardesty. I pictured Woody's foxy eyes and remembered this fact about foxes: they didn't *chew* their food, they *shredded* it with their sharp teeth and swallowed it.

I shook my head. If there was one huge lesson for me it was this: *you have to trust your own instincts first.* I should have stuck with my gut feeling about Woody 'cause I was sure now that besides his gambling problem he was in some kind of trouble. He was probably one of those parents who stole his own kid. I'd tell Nora about him and we'd go online to check out those missing children sites.

I sat, cross-legged in the opening of my tent, making a fist and slamming it into the palm of my other hand. Over and over I did this as I stared out into the rain, waiting to see the headlights of his truck.

The slightest trace of dawn was seeping in under the clouds

when I finally heard his pickup rumble into the campsite. The rain had stopped, but it was damp and cold. I pushed myself up from where I'd sort of keeled over asleep and saw that Buddy was curled up beside me. Then I rubbed my arms to get warm while I kept my eyes glued to that pickup.

What a coward. What a *sneak*, I thought, watching Woody close the door to his cab softly before tiptoeing toward his tent.

"Stop right there!" I ordered, rushing to head him off.

Woody raised his hands like I'd drawn a gun on him. "Hey, I know what you're gonna say and you don't need to say it."

"Yeah? What is it you think I'm gonna say?"

"That I stole your money," Woody offered right away.

For a second, I was speechless. I never thought he'd admit to it.

"I *did* take it. I don't deny it," Woody went on quickly. "I took it so I could double what you had. Honest I did. We're all leaving soon—I wanted to make it easier for you."

What? Was this possible? . . . Nah, I doubted it.

"So how much did you make for me?" I asked. "I had seven hundred and thirty-five dollars in that sock."

He brought his arms down. "Well, that's the thing."

"What's the *thing*?" I demanded.

Woody motioned to the picnic table. "Look, can we sit? Let me explain."

Undecided, but skeptical, I stood, clenching my hands while Woody sat at the table.

"Look," he said, "I got nine hundred dollars tied up in a private poker game back there in Charles Town. All of us in the game, we took a break to get some rest. We're goin' back this afternoon to finish. I'll get your money back and I'll double it, I promise."

"You're a liar!" I accused him. "People don't stop poker games halfway to catch a nap. You frickin' stole my money and lost it, didn't you?"

"I told you, I've got it tied up in a game!"

I took another step forward and pulled my right arm back but as I did, Woody jumped up from the table and hammered me first. A fast, right-handed jab into my jaw sent me spinning to the ground. In no time flat, Woody was on my back, yanking my arms behind me so hard it made me wince.

"Don't do you no good to come after me!" he growled into my ear. "I can take you down nothin' flat, see? Make one wrong move and you're mincemeat."

His breath was hot and smelled like alcohol.

"Ain't nothin' you can do about that money," Woody said. "I told you. I'm goin' back this afternoon to get that money back. What choice do you have anyway? Huh? You *don't.* Because if you say a word to anybody, I'll have the cops in here so fast, *Michael Griswald,* you won't know what hit you."

I didn't say a thing. It felt like he broke my jaw, and I could barely breathe he was so heavy on my back. My lip was bleeding, too. I could taste the blood.

When he finally let go and stood up, he stunned the heck out of me by actually reaching a hand down to help me up. "I'm warning you," he said, "don't make a single move against me or you won't see a nickel of that money." His voice softened up. "Sorry this happened. You know I can't help myself. I told you. I'm gonna get your money back."

I swallowed hard and held my sore jaw.

Woody disappeared into his tent, leaving me to feel like a stupid, no-good sucker. I had no idea he was so strong—or so fast! I thought about sneaking into the tent while he was asleep and smashing a log over his head. But then I thought: what if Woody gambled again and won big? Would he bring some money back? I didn't care if he doubled it, I just wanted my $735 back—or part of it. I'd be happy with half. Heck, I'd settle for a hundred bucks!

That day was one of the worst I'd had in a while. While Woody slept, I got some ice out of the cooler and pressed it to my jaw. I was tired from not sleeping much and depressed as all get-out about my money.

When Luke got up, I helped him get breakfast. When he asked what happened to my face, I told him I fell. I tried again to sleep, but couldn't. When Woody stomped off early afternoon—without saying a word to anybody—I knew where he was going and could only hope his luck was better.

I would have told Nora, but it was Saturday and neither of us was working at the horse farm that day. She'd gone into town to use the café's computer to finish an English paper, and I was taking the day off in exchange for working the next day with her.

If I didn't get my money back, no way could I go with Nora and her mom to Las Vegas. I didn't want to depend on them for everything.

I have no memory of what else happened that afternoon, maybe on account of I was so tired and miserable. But after Luke and I had dinner—some tomato soup with cheese and crackers—we were sitting at the picnic table playing cards, kind of waiting for Woody to show up again. I do remember smelling smoke and looked to see if I put out the fire we'd made. Then a car come barreling down the camp road splashing through the puddles. Nora's mom screeched her car to a halt and Nora screamed out the window, "The horse barn's on fire!"

"Stay here with Buddy!" I ordered Luke. "Don't go anywhere!"

Running full speed, I threw myself into the backseat of Nora's mom's car. That woman sped over to the farm like a race car driver. If she ever got tired of training horses, I thought, she could get a job with NASCAR.

She turned the corner at the farm driveway and right off we got stopped by a big fire truck, a pumper, dropping hoses along the driveway and feeding them from the old cow pond on up to the barn. Nora and I jumped out of the car.

"You kids stay back!" a firefighter hollered at us.

We did like he said. We backed away, then we ducked behind the truck and sprinted up the lane toward the barn. We couldn't run fast enough 'cause we knew there were at least eight horses in the barn.

The fire was raging with orange flames and white smoke pouring into the night sky. It was daytime bright and so hot that from twenty feet back you could hardly stand it. We had to hold our arms up to shield the heat from our faces.

"Get that second pumper up here!" Firefighters had to yell

to one another in order to be heard above all the popping and crackling that fire made.

Frantic, high-pitched neighing sounds—like screams—came from the horses trapped inside the barn. You couldn't help but feel their terror. When we spotted Mrs. Crawford, an apron on, her hands on her face, we ran over to her.

"I don't know what happened!" she cried. "I was putting one of the grandkids to bed when I looked out the window and saw the flames!"

I had an idea of what happened though. "Did Miguel work today?"

She looked at me. "What?"

I yelled louder. "Did Miguel work today?"

"Yes!"

I knew it. Miguel's smoking started the fire.

"Why?" Mrs. Crawford grabbed my wrist. "What about Miguel?"

But just then, a firefighter came from the barn with the two little donkeys, Winston and Earl, trotting fast on either side of him. Mrs. Crawford rushed to grab the donkeys' halters and lead them to a side pasture. Another firefighter came through the smoke with this horse named Princess, and I ran to take her halter.

When I got back to Nora's side, another pumper was rumbling into place near the barn. It was followed by a second big tanker. Several firefighters pulled the end of a hose and rushed toward the barn. When a stream of water gushed out they directed it upwards, toward the hayloft.

"Do you have an adequate water supply from the pond?" the fire chief shouted into his radio. He stood in the whirring red light of his truck. "Is this thing going to jump to the house?"

"Why aren't they going in for more horses?" Nora hollered at me.

"I don't know!" I hollered back.

Just then an explosion blew off part of the barn roof and a fresh burst of flames jumped into the sky. Everyone scurried back as cinders flew like fireworks, some landing just a feet away from us. Seconds later, Dakota and three other horses tore out of the barn, wide-eyed and scared, their tails held high, their hooves pounding the ground. I sprang forward, arms outstretched to stop them from running down the driveway. At the same time, Nora's mom rushed up from the other direction and used her arms to herd the horses toward that side pasture.

Then Nora started to lose it. "Fuego's in there!" she cried.

"I know!" I was counting in my head: five horses out, the two donkeys. She was right; Fuego was still in the back with two others.

"Hurry up, hurry up!" I muttered out loud.

"Flames on the roof!" the fire chief shouted into his radio. "Flames on the roof! Everybody out! *Now!*"

"No!" Nora screamed. "No! Fuego's still in there!"

The firefighters with the hose rushed back out of the barn just as an entire wall collapsed. Turning around, the crew took aim again and shot water toward the hayloft from outside the barn. Another firefighter limped out of the smoky barn coughing, and two rescue workers rushed forward to help him.

I approached the fire chief. "What about the rest of the horses?" I yelled. "There's at least three of them still inside! They're in the back!"

"No one's going in there now!" he shouted. "No building integrity! The roof's going to cave in any second!"

"Nooooo!" Nora cried from behind me. Her hands were two fists at her mouth. Tears pooled in her eyes.

My heart pounded in my chest. I had a soft spot for that ole stallion myself. I didn't want him to die a miserable death. Quickly, I walked Nora back a ways where she could hear without me yelling. "Stay here, okay?"

"Why? What are you doing?"

"Just stay here!" I repeated firmly. I put an arm up to protect my face and ran toward the barn, but in no time, the heat was so intense it stopped me like a wall. I felt someone grab me by the arm and yank me backward.

I got dropped on the ground and a firefighter pointed his gloved finger at me. "Where do you think you're going?" he hollered at me. "You stay out of there!"

"Okay!" I told him, holding up a hand. "Okay."

But as soon as he turned, I got up, brushed myself off, and sauntered away—and around, into the shadows. I checked to be sure Nora wasn't following me, then I dashed behind the barn. The doors were locked from the inside, but I knew the tack room had a window. I picked up a brick and threw it at the window, shattering it. Then I grabbed an old bench, pulled it over, and used it to stand on so I could kick out the rest of the glass and get inside.

It was dark and smoke was beginning to roll in. Rushing over to the sink in the tack room, I turned on the water. Then I yanked off my sweatshirt and my long-sleeved T-shirt, which I soaked under the faucet. I put the sweatshirt back on and, holding the wet shirt over my face, felt my way past the shelves I'd made into the central hallway.

My heart beat double time high in my chest. Already I had trouble breathing. The swirling smoke was rapidly filling the barn. But what happens is that smoke and fire gases rise until they get stopped by a ceiling or a roof. They kind of hover there and go horizontal before they fall back down. We'd just learned this—in this very barn! If you got low you could still find air. So I squatted and, walking like a duck, made my way down the hallway, one hand against the wall, the other pressing the wet T-shirt to my face. I heard Fuego shriek and kick the wall. The other horses were frantic, too. They made a desperate noise I'll never forget and the floor shook from their crazed, heavy hooves.

I duckwalked my way to one door, reached up, pushed the bolt to one side, and flung open the door. A white horse named Nugget charged out and ran toward the front door.

The stall next door to Nugget was a pinto named Diablo. I opened his stall, too, then sat back on my heels to keep from getting trampled. But no horse ran out and I couldn't see through the smoke. "Come on!" I hollered, but I couldn't wait.

Fuego was in the stall across from Diablo. I made my way over, reached up, slid the bolt, and pushed open the door. "Fuego! Go, man! Run for your life!"

But he didn't come. I couldn't see him, but I heard his terrified noises just a few feet away. I remembered us learning that in a fire horses might be too scared to leave their stalls. They'd want to stay in the last safe place they knew, which is why we might have to cover their faces and lead them out.

It was hard to breathe, let alone see, but I stepped deeper into Fuego's stall. One hand on the wall, I inched forward until I saw the horse in front of me, backed into the corner. He neighed and pawed at the floor. Did he know I was there?

"Fuego! Hey, boy!" I was struggling to breathe and my heart couldn't beat any faster. "It's me!" I said, my words muffled by the wet shirt. I took it away. "It's me!" I said, trying to sound calm. "Let's get you out of here! Okay, boy?"

It was crazy talk, but it helped get me close enough to throw my shirt over his eyes. I grabbed the material underneath and held on tight when he reared up. I was lifted off the ground and my feet came down with his and I had to sidestep fast so's not to get stomped on.

With the same hand that held the shirt over Fuego's face I grabbed the edge of his halter and tightened my grip. "Come on!"

But Fuego pulled back, planted his feet, and froze like a statue.

"Come on!" I hollered. "Move!" I jerked on his halter.

Suddenly, the horse reared up a second time. I had to let

go and fell to the floor. I scrambled in the hay and manure to get away from his hooves. But when I tried to push myself up I couldn't. I had no strength and couldn't catch my breath. Smoke was everywhere then, burning my eyes, stinging my lungs. I was dizzy and for a second, I forgot where I was. I knew one of those poisonous fire gases could knock you out flat. It's what killed a lot of people in fires. Desperate, I covered my nose with one hand and forced myself to crawl out of there. In the hallway, bright new flames ate up the wall near the tack room so I veered left. On my feet, but hunched over, I inched my way, low along the wall, in smoky darkness.

Somehow I made it to the front doors, where I collapsed. A firefighter ran up and dragged me over to the side. "I told you not to go in there!"

While I sucked in air, he shouted. "We need oxygen over here!"

Clear, sweet air.

"You okay?"

I was coughing so hard I couldn't answer.

He would never understand, but that firefighter must have had half a heart. He roughed up my hair and said, "You did a helluva job, kid. You got the last two out. But you're a stupid son of a B, you know that?"

Turns out I didn't need that oxygen. Just some fresh air. Lots of it.

"Did that . . . that stallion come out?" I managed to ask him.

"The pinto? The black and white? Like a rocket!"

"No. No, the stallion. He's reddish with a gold mane."

"I'm not sure." He shook his head. "The other one was white."

I tugged on the edge of his coat. "He's still in there then!"

The firefighter kneeled beside me. "You need to call it quits, son." He gave me a bottle of water. I squeezed my eyes shut. I drank the water. I coughed hard.

And fresh tears soothed my burning eyes.

There wasn't anything else I could do but watch, and wait. A few minutes later, I looked across the fire-lit yard and saw Miguel. Our eyes met and when they did, he turned on his heel. I got up, brushed hay and manure off my hands, and started to follow him.

Suddenly, an explosion shook the ground. Another huge burst of flames shot skyward and sideways, sending sparks and cinders in all directions as the entire barn caved in. Knowing there was one horse that didn't make it out, it felt like my heart caved in, too. I caught sight of Nora then. A few feet away, she held her head and cried for Fuego.

Sadness quickly turned to anger as I swung my head around and searched for Miguel again. I saw him lifting the bike he always rode to the farm. But he didn't make it onto that bike because I got there fast and tackled him from behind.

We sailed over his bike and hit the ground hard, then rolled, over and over, across the dirt driveway and onto the grass. When we stopped, I let him go and as he turned over, I balled up my fist and smacked him one. I knew I'd busted his nose. Blood spurted all over and he never fought back.

"That'll teach you to smoke cigarettes at this farm!" I hollered at him.

When I walked away, Miguel was on his knees, his bloody hands clutching his face.

Returning to the crowd, I saw Mrs. Crawford coming toward me. She gave me a hug. "Thank you so much, Gerry," she said. She hadn't seen the fight, only my effort at getting the last three horses out. "It's all my fault," she kept saying. "It was the hay in the loft. All my fault!"

I put an arm around her shoulders. "It wasn't your fault!" I told her. "It was Miguel. He's been smoking!"

"No. No. The fire started in the loft where we stacked the wet hay."

Nora came over.

"Tell her, Nora. It's not her fault. Miguel's been smoking."

Nora wiped tears off her cheeks with the palms of both hands. "The fire chief says it was the wet hay."

"What are you guys talking about?"

"The fire started in the loft where you boys stacked the wet hay." Mrs. Crawford leaned toward me. "We never should have stacked it before it dried."

"I know! I told you that!"

"*So*, why don't you stack wet hay?" Nora still had to yell to be heard.

I shrugged. I didn't know. Why were they asking? "Because it'll rot?"

"No! Because when it dries and cures, it creates heat!" Nora shouted. "The wet hay stacked in the loft caused the fire. It's called spontaneous combustion!"

CHAPTER TWENTY-THREE

KEEP RUNNING

I felt like such a loser. A complete and total loser.

First, I had risked my life and had zero to show for it, except how stupid I looked. Then I'd punched out Miguel for *nothing* which was proof positive that I could never change. When I get angry, I lash out. It's just who I am.

In the past, none of these things would have bothered me a lick. I would have figured, what the heck, it was just a dumb horse that died. And Miguel? He had it coming anyway! But something inside of me shifted that night. I'd gone from driving hard to neutral, and I was coasting downhill on an empty tank. . . .

Exhausted and numb, I stood in a pasture in the eerie half-light from the dying fire, running my fingers through Diablo's black and white coat to be sure no lingering cinders burned his skin. Beside me, Nora searched for burning embers on the two donkeys.

We stayed at the farm for hours after most people left, tending to the horses while one fire crew remained to hose down what was left of the barn. A couple firefighters walked around kicking the blackened clumps of hay apart, soaking all of it so the fire wouldn't start again. I'd overheard one of them say if they hadn't been together at the firehouse having their chicken barbecue, they wouldn't have gotten there in time to save any of the horses. They were volunteers after all. Normally, they'd rush to the firehouse when they heard the siren go off.

Nora cried hard about Fuego. Afterward, she was quiet while we sat together on a bench near the farm's parking lot. "It's because Fuego didn't trust anyone," she said finally. "Remember what they told us? That stall was the last safe place he knew and he wasn't going to leave it."

I nodded. "Yeah, I remember."

"A little more time," Nora kept saying. "He just needed a little more time."

She was right. But that horse was still so mad at the world that he couldn't trust the one human being who came to save him. I understood—I really did. He was backed into a corner feeling there was no way out. I even wondered if people—if kids like me—could be the same way. Not trust anybody and so never take a chance on change, just stay on the same path to nowhere 'cause it's the only path they knew.

When Mrs. Crawford found us sitting on the bench and asked for help in checking the horses for cinders we got up right away. While we walked toward the paddock I said how sorry I was I couldn't save Fuego. "I tried," I told Mrs. Crawford. "I really tried."

She stopped and touched my arm. "I know you did! Sometimes that's all we can do is try, Gerry. But look, as far as I'm concerned you were a hero tonight—even though you *never* should have gone back in that barn the way you did. We lost Fuego, yes, but we have Nugget and Diablo."

It's true. At least I saved those guys.

The three of us walked on and Nora asked Mrs. Crawford what would happen to the horses now.

"I've got some volunteers with barn space," she replied. "The others can stay out in the pasture until I find homes."

Later, I wondered what would happen to *me*. Pretty obvious my work at the farm was over. No job and a lot of guilt for busting Miguel's nose.

When I finished going over every inch of Diablo that night, I moved the lantern that was giving me some light and helped Nora finish one of the donkeys.

"Have you found any hot spots?" I asked.

"Actually, I did," Nora said. "Two cinders on Earl."

We worked in silence for a moment.

"You're still coming with us, aren't you?" Nora asked.

I lifted my shoulders and let them fall. "I don't know."

"You have to," Nora said, disappearing as she examined the donkey's leg all the way down to his hoof. "There's nothing for you here anymore."

"It won't feel right, Nora. I don't have any money to contribute."

"What about all the money you saved?"

"Woody stole it."

Nora's head popped up. "What?!"

"Woody stole it all and gambled it away."

"When?"

"Sometime yesterday."

"No way!" Nora was pretty horrified. "What a crook!"

"Yeah. That's what I said."

She narrowed her eyes. "He's addicted, you know. Gamblers, they get addicted to it and they can't stop. I'll bet it's at the heart of all his problems."

"Yeah, well, it's kind of at the heart of my problems right now, too, 'cause I don't have a red cent. It's not his only problem either," I went on. "I never told you this, Nora, but I found out ole Woody is using a fake name. And so is Luke. They're running from something."

"From what?"

"I don't know. I could be wrong, but I think Woody is one of those parents who kidnaps his own kid, you know what I mean?"

"Oh, my gosh. That would make sense, though, wouldn't it? Luke told me once that he wasn't allowed to talk about his mother. We should have gone online and checked the missing kids site!"

"I know. We still can," I said. "I also thought of saying something to Luke's teacher. Seems like she really cares about him. She could take the information to the police."

"We'll write that note together, Dig. Before we leave for Nevada next week."

I let my eyes drop. I didn't want to tell her again that I couldn't go. Not without any money of my own.

"Guess I'm right back where I started when I first got here," I said instead. "I don't have nothin' except a few new clothes and a dog I never wanted."

Nora reached over the donkey's back and took my hands. "I disagree," she said, forcing me to look at her again. "Remember how down and out you were with all that poison ivy on your face? Look at you now! You're strong. You're healthy! Maybe you don't have the money you earned, but you have *me*!"

I had to smile at that, and I squeezed her hands.

"You've got a tough shell, Dig, but there's a good heart underneath it. And you know what?"

She waited until our eyes met.

"What?"

"Two things. First, you really need a haircut, which I'm happy to do. And second," she said, pausing just a bit, "I wanted to tell you that I love you." The corners of her mouth lifted when she said that and shadowy light from the lantern reflected off her sooty, tear-stained cheeks.

What a night, I thought. I squeezed her hands again, then lifted them up to my face and kissed her knuckles.

By the time I finally returned to the campsite, it was Sunday morning. I was pretty wiped out.

Luke was waiting. "What happened?" he asked, rushing down the road to meet me, Buddy at his heels.

I told him all about the fire, but said we got the horses out in time. I didn't see any point in telling him about Fuego—or what I did to Miguel.

"Is your dad back?"

Luke shook his head no.

"Well. Don't worry." I begged Luke then to let me sleep for a while. "Think you can hang out with Buddy?"

When Luke said "sure" I crawled into my tent to sleep.

I didn't hear Woody's truck when he came back that afternoon. Nor any of the police cars that pulled in after it. That's how deep asleep I was.

"Wake up!" Luke said urgently, shaking my shoulder. "Wake up!"

Startled, I rolled over and sat up. *Now what?* I wondered.

"The police are here! I'm scared!"

I peered out through the tent opening and saw it was daylight. I also caught a glimpse of Woody's truck with red and white lights blinking behind it.

Unbelievable. I sprang out of bed, grabbed my boots, and hightailed it out of the tent, through the campground, and down the path that went to the river. At the shoreline, when I paused to pull my boots on, I could hear a police radio crackle. I figured I'd cross the river again by hopping the boulders. Police didn't look for me there the last time; maybe it would work again.

The water was up in the river, deep, dark, and cold as it rushed around the boulders. I was extra careful as I jumped from one rock to the next. When I got to the far side, I looked back. I didn't see anyone following me so I sat down to figure out my next step. Good thing I'd slept in my clothes, I thought, just then realizing how much they smelled like smoke. I patted my pants pockets. The jackknife was still there and in the other pocket, the news article and the white card from Cliffside. It was wet, and on the back side, the only words you could read were the first four: *I will help others* . . .

Weird how things happen sometimes. I read that, then I glanced back across the river and saw Luke and Buddy about a third of the way across, hopping from rock to rock.

I jumped to my feet. Couldn't he see how high and fast the water was? One slip and he'd be swept away.

"Go back, Luke!" I yelled from the shoreline. "Go back!"

But he didn't. Then I remembered he couldn't swim. I never did give him those swimming lessons. I didn't even think about what to do next. I ran back over the rocks, hollering, "Luke, stop!"

We met about halfway and I grabbed him by the arm.

"What the hell are you doing?" I screamed at him.

Luke was crying. "Going with you. I'm scared."

"Scared? Of what?"

"The police that came took my daddy."

"They took *Woody*?" Why would they take Woody? And did that mean they weren't after me?

"They put handcuffs on him," Luke said. "The police said he robbed the gas station. When they put him in the backseat of the police car, I ran away."

I rolled my eyes and wondered if Woody was after more gambling money—or was he trying to get money to pay me back? Who knew?

"Well, you can't come with *me*," I declared. "They'll think

I kidnapped you, Luke. I'll be in worse trouble than I am now!"

Luke was shaking his head. "No. I don't want to go back. I want to go home to my mom. I don't want to play adventure anymore."

"Adventure? Is that what this is? An adventure with your dad?"

"Yeah. That's why we have adventure names. Daddy says Mommy doesn't love me and doesn't care if I'm gone, but I want to go home."

"What's your real name?"

"It's Andrew."

"Look, Luke—*Andrew*, you've got to go back. I can't get you home to your mom. But the police can. Just tell them your real name and where you live."

"I live in Texas! I live in San Antonio, Texas!"

"Tell that to the police!"

"But what if they don't send me back?"

"What else would they do?"

Luke shrugged. "I don't know!"

"Go on!" I ordered him. *"Now!"*

But then I took another look at the water rushing past and decided I'd better be sure he made it all the way back. I held his hand and yikes, there were some spots he could barely jump across 'cause the water was so high. I never let go of his hand though. When we landed on dry ground, I gave him a hug and said I needed to go.

Buddy followed me, although he seemed confused. So was

I, to be honest. I didn't know where I was going, or why I was going—or what I was going to do when I got there! I mean, I hadn't even said good-bye to Nora. And I didn't have a penny to my name, just the ruined white card and a stolen jackknife.

But what else could I do?

Hopping from rock to rock, I retraced those sketchy steps back across the raging river. I guess 'cause the only thing I knew how to do was to keep running.

CHAPTER TWENTY-FOUR

NOT AGAIN

Landing on the opposite side of the river from Luke, I paused a moment, hands on my hips, 'cause honest, I did not know what to do. Buddy, panting hard, gazed up at me and I kneeled to pet him while the questions hammered me.

Would I head home now, to protect my mom and the kids? How? How would I deal with my father? And how would I live 'cause I'd always have to hide?

Should I wait until the coast was clear and go to Nevada with Nora and her mom after all? It would give me more time to think about things. But then, wasn't that just running, too? Running in a different direction?

Like a pile driver, the questions beat on me until I felt reduced to a million little pieces. I was totally blanked on what to do and the running had plumb wore me out. I was so desperate for direction, some sort of sign for what to do that I stood up again and gazed back at the river. And that's when a living nightmare unfolded right before my eyes.

Luke hadn't stayed where I left him! He was following me

again, only this time someone was after him! A police officer was trying to catch him, but had stopped jumping the rocks, probably because he was too fat and loaded down with gear. Instead, the cop stood talking to somebody on his police radio while Luke got farther out into the river.

I knew yelling would give me away. I knew when I opened my mouth it was all over. But I could not let Luke put himself in that kind of danger.

"Stop!" I shouted. "Luke, stop!" Even if Luke wasn't his real name, I wasn't gonna change it then. "Go back!"

Unbelievable, but the dumb kid kept coming.

Buddy barked at me, like *go get him*! But I wasn't sure whether to cross the river again and get caught, or hope Luke would freak out and stop so the cop could catch up. Voices battled in my head: *such a loser . . . sometimes all you can do is try . . . you'll look stupid.* And in that split second of indecision I saw Luke miss the edge of a rock and fall in the water. Instantly, he was sucked under and went flying with the rushing water between two boulders. His little head popped up several feet away already, but I knew he couldn't last long out there.

The nightmare that haunted my life was happening *again*— with another little boy! No way. No way would I let it happen a second time!

I yanked off my boots and sprinted back across the rocks. When I saw a place that looked like deep water, I took a chance and dove in—a shallow dive so I wouldn't hit rocks underneath. The water was ice-cold and moving fast. As soon as I surfaced, I caught a glimpse of Luke's head downriver and swam like crazy. The sweatshirt was weighing me down some, but the current was with me so I closed in pretty quick. I grabbed for Luke but he disappeared inches from my hands! When his head didn't pop up again, I went under after him.

The river was dark, full and fast because of the recent rain. The currents were unmerciful, some pulling this way, some that. Forget *seeing* anything. All I could do was reach out my arms and flail around in the churning water, feeling for him. If I hadn't collided with him the way I did, it would've been over for sure. When I felt his arm, I grabbed it and latched on.

I resurfaced, gasping for breath, and pulled him up with me. Then I got my arm over his chest and turned over on my back so I could float and keep him up.

Luke coughed—a good sound—while together, we went flying down a chute of wild rapids in the cold, rushing river.

Rocks battered my back like it was a punching bag. Then my head slammed into another boulder, nearly knocking me out. Silver stars were all I saw. I felt my grip letting go. But, no! I couldn't lose him! I squeezed Luke tighter and focused on keeping that one arm around him.

The rapids continued, fast and cruel. I held on to Luke with everything I had until the water finally slowed down. "Luke, you okay?" I tried to shout.

No answer. I couldn't see his face. But he had latched on to my arm with both hands and was holding on tight.

I knew I'd cut my head, but the only pain I felt was from the icy water.

Finally, we hit a calm stretch. No more rocks or rapids, just smooth, cold, fast-moving river. Buddy ran along the bank on the Virginia side, following us and barking his head off.

I looked toward the Maryland side and saw the campground's boat launch come and go. Red and white police car lights flashed while two officers walked along the water's edge, probably looking for Luke. I saw a guy point and holler, but I couldn't hear anything. I think my ears were still ringing from my head getting smashed.

When the river took a turn and the water slowed even more, I started kicking and backpedaling with one arm as hard as I could toward the Maryland shoreline. It was a pretty sorry one-handed backstroke, but it got us over to the edge where there was a shallow, sandy bank. Exhausted and shaking from the cold, I got both feet on the sandy bottom and hauled Luke up on shore where I turned him on his side. He coughed and sputtered and water dribbled out of his mouth so I knew he was okay.

I reached up to wipe the blood off my face, then felt the ragged edges of flesh on my scalp where I'd sliced it open. I pressed one hand against the wound to try and stop the bleeding, then knelt on the sand and sucked in huge amounts of air. When Luke threw up, I put a hand on his back. "Get it all out, Luke. You're doin' good."

Had we been in the water a minute? Five minutes? Who knew? It seemed like forever.

One other thought crossed my mind: was this what it was like for Brady? When he pulled Ben out of the river?

Suddenly, Buddy was there, licking my hands and Luke's face. He was wet from swimming across the river and when he shook, he sprayed us both with water, but we didn't care.

Still catching my breath, I leaned in close to Luke. "Hey, dude. You okay?"

"Yeah. I think so . . . thanks . . . for saving me."

When he said that I moved my head back and forth. "No," I said to him, and this I meant: "Thanks for saving *me*."

It didn't take long for the police to find us. They put Luke on a stretcher but he called for me so I went over to him. I took his hand in both of mine.

His face was all screwed up. "I lost my glasses," he said.

I almost laughed. "Don't worry about it," I said. "You'll get some new ones."

Then I turned to one of the cops. "His name is Andrew Hardesty. His father's real name is Glen David Hardesty. They're from San Antonio, Texas."

Another officer held up a small notebook. "We got that much from the father. We'll take care of getting the boy home to his mother, where he belongs."

Good. I was glad Woody had confessed to the truth.

I looked down at Luke. "You hear that?"

He nodded.

"You'll be all right now, Luke." I let go of his hand. "Take care of yourself. And keep practicin' those layups, you hear?"

He grinned.

———————

Turning away, I took off my sweatshirt and even though it was sopping wet, I used it to try and stop the bleeding from my head. I sat down again on the beach and Buddy came over to stand beside me. Soon, a police officer was there, too. He moved my hand away so he could see the wound. "Looks like you might need some stitches," he said.

I didn't respond. It almost didn't matter if I bled to death, right then and there. The important thing was that Luke was all right.

"What's your name, son?"

I didn't hesitate. "Michael Griswald," I told him.

Someone put a blanket around my shoulders and I held it close together with one hand. I was wet from head to toe, and *freezing*. I bet I didn't smell like smoke anymore.

While the cop talked into his police radio, I saw Nora. Her hair was loose and she held a hand over her heart like she was breathing hard from running. I got up and went to her. She hugged me even though I was wet so I dropped the sweatshirt *and* the blanket and wrapped both my arms around her, too.

"I'm sorry," I whispered in her ear. "You and me, it wasn't gonna work for us to be running away, or me going to Las Vegas."

She pressed her head into my shoulder.

"I gotta go back and do my time, Nora. And you gotta go with your mom and stay in school. You can't be a doctor if you drop out, right?"

She moved her head in agreement.

"We can stay in touch if you want. Who knows? Maybe we'll meet up again someday," I said. "But both of us, we got stuff to do first."

"I know," Nora said. "I know . . ."

Suddenly, a cop was there handing me a towel for my head and saying, "You did a brave thing, Michael. I'm sorry I have to take you in now."

Reluctantly, I pulled away from Nora.

"The report here says you've been on the run for two months," the cop said. "But it's over now."

I put the towel against my head and nodded. "I'm glad."

CHAPTER TWENTY-FIVE

RESTITUTION

restitution (res´ ta too´ shan) *n.* 1. a giving back to the rightful owner of something that has been lost or taken away; restoration; 2. a making good for loss or damage; reimbursement.

In the waiting room at the prison's medical clinic, there was a bunch of stuff on the coffee table: a Bible, a copy of *Sports Illustrated* with the cover ripped off, a *People* magazine, and a dictionary. While I waited to get the twenty stitches out of my scalp, I hobbled over and picked up the dictionary—no small task when you're in handcuffs and your feet are shackled. But I wanted to look up the word my public defender had used so many times: *restitution*. The word that was going to keep me from ever realizing my dreams.

I guess I always thought I'd go straight back to Cliffside when I got caught, but that's not what happened. I went in a police car to the hospital where the gash on my head got stitched up, then I went straight to a small prison in this place called Hagerstown. It wasn't anything like Cliffside, which is in the mountains with no real fence around it. When we drove into this Hagerstown prison, I caught a glimpse of a high brown concrete wall with razor wire all around the top of it.

After getting buzzed in, I shuffled a few steps with my handcuffs and shackles. Then I had to wait for a guard to punch in a code to open another door. There was a solid, mechanical clunk when the lock released and the door opened. I shuffled some more, another clunk, then I shuffled again down the hallway to where they put me in a tiny, one-room cell about the size of a closet. The cell didn't have anything but a stainless steel sink and toilet, a metal cot with a thin mattress and some bedding rolled up tight at one end. No window to look out of, just a tiny rectangle of glass in the door.

"Thirty days in the hole," one guard told me. So I guessed that cell was going to be my home for a while, until the court decided where I got sent, and how much more time they would tack on.

Didn't matter to me anymore what they did. After everything that happened, I almost didn't care. I was thinking I'd just do my time and try to move forward with my life. For sure, I was relieved to be done running.

A couple days later, this public defender guy came to see me. He said he was Timothy Joseph, which struck me weird, like having two first names for a name. He seemed too young to be a lawyer, but he was nice and acted like he cared. He brought me a can of Coke and didn't seem rushed.

"I'm going to represent you in court, Michael," he said. "So, it's important that you tell me everything about your life. From the beginning, okay?"

I figured I would cooperate. What the heck, I didn't have anything to lose at that point and I was still in limbo land, wondering what they would do to me.

First off, I told him, "Don't call me Michael. Everybody calls me Digger."

"Okay, Digger. Tell me your story."

So I took a big breath and I told him my story. I told him about growing up on the Eastern Shore of Maryland, my friends J.T. and Brady, my mom, LeeAnn, and Hank. I even told Mr. Joseph some of the stuff my father did to me and my mom over the years so he had the whole picture and understood why I run away from Cliffside in the first place. Being a public defender he already had papers that told him about the red kayak, and how Ben DiAngelo died, so I didn't need to go into that again. But I did tell him how I still carried the weight from it, and how I knew I always would.

"That's one thing I learned for sure living out there these past two months," I said. "No matter how far I run, or how long I'm gone, I'll never get away from that weight 'cause it's part of who I am.

"I thought a lot about this," I said, "and I decided that the only thing I can do is live a decent life to try and make up for all the wrong I did. Maybe the weight will get a little lighter, but that's about all I can hope for."

Mr. Joseph tilted his head and nodded slowly. "I think that's a real good way to look at it."

"Yeah. I just hope that I can have like a halfway normal life, too," I added.

"You have a long life in front of you, Digger. And it can be a good one—even with the weight you carry. It's up to you how you shape that life. Have you ever thought of what you might want to do? Do you have any goals? Any dreams?"

My head had been kind of hanging down the whole time I talked, but I looked up then. "I don't know that it's possible what with all I've done," I said. "But I'd like to join the Marines one day."

His eyebrows went up, like he was impressed with that idea, but he didn't say anything for a few seconds. I knew what the hesitation meant. He didn't even have to tell me, but he did.

"The Marines, well . . ." He cleared his throat. "Unfortunately I don't think so, Digger. You've already had one felony conviction—the second-degree murder charge that put you at Cliffside. Now you're facing felony theft for stealing the truck. That'll be two felonies on your record. The Marines are not going to look the other way on that."

Even though I was expecting that kind of answer, it still hit me hard.

"No chance then?" I had to ask. "For me to *ever* be a Marine?"

He shook his head. "I'm sorry." Then he added: "When you screw up, it has consequences."

That seemed kind of harsh, but it was true, I guess. My eyes fell away from his. I stared down at the dirty, scuffed-up tile near my feet as my dream seeped out and disappeared, leaving a hollow feeling inside. All those years I had that dream. Now it was gone.

"Look," Mr. Joseph said. He leaned forward and put his hands on the table between us. "A lot of people have to change their dreams, Digger. Things happen. You adjust. You have to roll a little with life."

He opened his hands. "So you're not a Marine! There are lots of other things you can do. You're strong. You're smart. And you know what? Inside that tough shell you carry around, you've got a good heart. I'm telling you, that can take you far in this world."

It was almost exactly what Nora had said to me. I don't think he noticed, but I winced a little 'cause Mr. Joseph had poked the tender spot I nursed deep inside for Nora. Would I ever even see her again? Would she write to me?

My public defender leaned back in his chair and opened my file on one of his crossed legs. "I'm hoping the court will take a lot of factors into consideration and not give you too much more time."

I sat there, unfeeling, as he thumbed through my papers.

"At least you didn't commit any violent acts while you were on the run."

"Well, except for I hit this guy, Miguel." If a lawyer was examining my life he might as well know everything. "I punched him out good. I think I may have broke his nose."

He frowned at me. "I didn't see anything about a fight . . ."

"No, probably not. Miguel's an illegal, you know? He probably didn't want to bring attention to himself by reporting it."

Mr. Joseph didn't comment. Quietly, he closed my file. Guess he didn't want to get involved with that. Not that I cared much then, but it bothered me later on that we both kind of brushed it aside.

"Look, Digger," he said, "the point here is that we tell your story in court. We say you're sorry, that you've changed and that you're—why are you smiling?"

"'Cause you said that I changed."

"Why is that funny?"

I shrugged. "'Cause I guess I didn't think I *could* change."

He didn't even blink. "Of course you changed! I mean, you could have kept on running, but you didn't. You didn't have to jump in that cold river. You didn't have to risk your life saving those horses in the barn fire. You didn't have to take such good care of Andrew, or Luke, or whatever his name is. All these things—they were totally selfless acts. You're a different person now! You matured!"

I thought about that and I don't know about *matured*, but I *was* changed some. I stopped running at least, and it's true, I did look at things different.

He continued, "So we talk about how you've changed and how you're ready to serve your time and pay restitution for the damage you did. Authorities recovered the stolen bicycle and the canoe, but the big thing is damage to that tractor-trailer truck."

At first, I thought what he meant was that I'd have to serve more time for stealing the truck and burning it up. But then I looked up the word in the dictionary when I was at the clinic, and the next time I saw Mr. Joseph he made it clear what restitution meant. It meant I would be held responsible for actually paying for the damage I done—*paying*, as in *money*.

"I did some research," Mr. Joseph said, picking up a legal pad with notes. "A tire on a tractor-trailer can cost from three hundred and fifty to six hundred dollars. That's for standard width. The new Michelin X One tire, which is twice as wide, is a bit more, so we'll have to find out what kind of tires were on that truck. From what I see you pretty much burned up all eighteen tires as well as the cab."

Wow. Math was never my strong point but if I ruined all the tires, then three hundred and fifty dollars times eighteen wheels was a big number—thousands of dollars—and that was just the minimum. It would take me years to come up with that kind of cash.

I shook my head sadly. How could I ever start over and have a life if I owed all that money? What was the point in even trying to find another dream?

CHAPTER TWENTY-SIX

A RAINBOW

While I was "in the hole" in Hagerstown, I had two other visitors. One was my Cliffside counselor, Mr. R. They brought me to wait for him in a small room that had a table and two chairs, and one poster on the wall with just words: YOU CAN'T CHANGE THE PAST BUT YOU CAN CHANGE THE FUTURE. I crossed my arms and stared at it, wondering if that could possibly be true.

When Mr. R. came in, I stood up. I didn't know if he'd shake my hand or come round to give me a big ole hug or what. But he didn't do any of that. He just pulled out a chair to sit down. So I did, too. Then I whipped out my white card and grinned when I showed it to him. "I had it with me the whole time."

Mr. R. didn't think that was funny. He didn't even crack a smile. "The thing is, Digger, what did you learn from that card?"

I dropped the grin 'cause he was right. It wasn't a joke.

"I learned a lot more than you think," I said. "I made a mistake taking off like that. I'm sorry I put you to so much trouble."

"I was never concerned with you troubling me, Digger.

And you know what I've always said about mistakes—they're not all bad because that's how we find out who we are, by making mistakes. But I was worried about your safety and I wondered *why* you took off. I thought you were smarter than that. Running never accomplishes anything, unless you're training for a marathon."

"I hear ya," I said.

"Some of the other boys were concerned about you and why you ran, too. Genuinely concerned," Mr. R. said. "Your old friend, J.T., must have asked me every other day if there was any news."

I looked up, astonished about J.T. "Are you serious?"

"Totally. Even after his father passed away, J.T. kept asking about you."

"What?" My eyes got wide 'cause I didn't know anything about that. *"His father?"*

"A month ago," Mr. R. said. "They let J.T. go home for the funeral, but he had to come back to serve out his time." I put a hand over my face and closed my eyes, ashamed all over again. No way could I ever make this up to J.T.

Then I kind of spaced out and went on to have another thought: what if it had been *my* father who died? He'd be gone. He wouldn't be there anymore to beat on my mother and me. But then I wouldn't have a father anymore either, and somewhere, in the deepest, darkest, tiniest corner of my heart, there was an ache. I sat there, feeling that ache spread until it clenched up my heart. I didn't want to *not* have a father. I would never have said this out loud to no one—

no way—but I think I still wanted there to be the possibility of a day when my father and me could be like a real father and son again. Like we were a long time ago driving the rig all those days and nights with hay or watermelons or frozen chickens stacked up in the trailer behind us.

Miracles still happen. Don't they? Maybe someday my father would actually say he was sorry. If I could change, maybe he could, too. Then I'd forgive him and we could all move on and like, be a family. It was then—thinking about this—that I realized I could never have seriously hurt my dad. It had always been in the back of my mind that I'd have to shoot him or bonk him over the head or something to protect my mom and the kids. But no matter how angry I got at my dad, there's no way on earth I could seriously take him down . . . especially not after Ben. Not after all that. Not ever.

So all that running I did? It wasn't me running home to get rid of my dad, or even to protect Mom and the kids. No. It was me running away from all the stuff in my head. All the guilt, all the anger, all the regret . . . I was like that dog Woody talked about, the dog with the kite tied to his tail. He kept running away from it but it was always going to be there.

When Mr. R. saw how quiet I got, then how upset I was, and how I pushed the heels of both my hands against my eyes and started crying, he softened up some and came round the table. He even put his arm around my shoulders. He kept saying it wasn't my fault J.T.'s father didn't get a kidney in time and died. No one could blame me for that. But we all knew it *was* my fault J.T. couldn't go home to help his family now when they needed him the most, which, truth be known, was not the reason I was crying.

Mr. R. and me, we sat there for a long time. Eventually, we had us a good talk about putting yesterday behind and starting over, taking each day one at a time. We talked about watching the ole temper, keeping my fists in check 'cause violence was never the answer to anything no matter how angry you got. We talked about staying out of trouble by avoiding negative people like my old friend Tio, and the boys in gangs. And we talked about me working hard in school so I'd have a future. Neither one of us ever mentioned my dad.

When we finished up, Mr. R. asked if there was anything he could do for me. At first I didn't think so, but then I told him, "Yes."

"If it's not a big deal, or too much out of your way, I wonder if you could check on that dog that was with me the past two months. Like maybe see if he got taken care of, or whatever. The officer, that day I got taken in, he said he'd take Buddy to the pound."

"Sure. I can try to find out for you," Mr. R. promised.

The other visitor I had was my mom. She drove up to see me again only this time she looked a lot better than the time before. She didn't have makeup caked on her face hiding some bruise. She hugged me long and hard and her eyes watered up. "I thought I'd lost you for good," she told me. "Grampa sends his love. I saw him at the nursing home yesterday. He wants you to come home." After she let go, she pulled out of her purse a little Ziploc bag full of my favorite minia-ture Snickers bars. "Hank set 'em aside from his Halloween loot," she said. "And here, this is for you, too." She gave me a picture LeeAnn had drawn and colored in with crayons. The picture was a rainbow with me on one side (I was a stick figure holding a basketball) and home at the other end (a house and three stick figures which I took to be LeeAnn, Hank, and Mom. They had big smiles and held flowers, except for LeeAnn who, Mom pointed out, was not holding a big pizza like I thought, but a plate of chocolate chip cookies).

"We're doing okay," my mother said as we both sat down. "We're back in the house, you know. And hey! We got the toilet fixed!"

I smiled some. I had to smile after hearing that.

My mom went on, more serious. "I got the court to give me a restraining order so your dad ain't been a bother to us. He's living over to Church Hill with your uncle Chip. I know what you told the public defender, Digger, that you run away from that juvenile detention center to get home and protect us. But you gotta know, hon, that there's nothin' you can do to fix that situation. That's for us adults to fix, not you. I'm tryin' hard, I really am. And like I said, I think I'm doin' better. You need to take care of yourself. Do your time and come on home to us."

All those days sitting in that cell alone I had a lot of time to think about what Mom said. I thought a lot about Nora, too. I wondered what it was like in Las Vegas. Was it hot every day? I hoped she was in a good high school 'cause she sure was smart. School would keep her going. It was her ticket out, no question. I thought about Luke (I just couldn't think of him as Andrew) getting reunited with his mother, and Mrs. Crawford finding places for all the horses. I thought about a red-colored stallion, too, a horse with a shaggy forelock and a nose like velvet, and wished he had taken a chance on me.

I didn't waste much time thinking about Woody. I figured he was where he belonged. But you know what? I hoped that someday he could change, too, 'cause I knew he really loved his son and for sure he'd want to see him again.

A lot of long, boring days with a lot of think time followed. Then Mr. R. surprised me by showing up a second time before my court appearance.

"I checked on your dog," he told me, "and he's already been adopted."

"No kidding," I said. I was happy Buddy found a home so soon, although I have to admit, there was a little pinch deep inside that hard heart of mine.

"Yeah," Mr. R. went on. "Some woman came in looking for that dog. Folks at animal control thought she'd lost it earlier because her little boy was so happy to see it. They couldn't give me any names, but the woman behind the desk said the people who adopted your dog were on their way to Texas."

A little smile had sprouted on my face when Mr. R. started telling me and it was full-blown by the time he finished.

When my day in court finally came, what they call my "dis-positional hearing," I was ready. I just wanted to get on with things. They shaved off the rest of my hair—everything they didn't shave when I got my stitches. And I was back in detention clothes: those blue Dickies pants and a white T-shirt and a navy blue sweatshirt, some clean socks to wear in my boots. Mr. Joseph had pretty much prepared me to get more time tacked on to a new, nine-month tour of duty. He thought that I'd be sent to a different detention center, too, and warned me that I'd be on AWOL watch for a while. That is, someone would be watching me 24/7 within an arm's reach, and I'd have to wear slippers instead of shoes. I guess so I wouldn't run.

In court, I listened to Mr. Joseph tell my sad story out loud. He pointed out how I didn't commit any violent acts and didn't carry a weapon. He made a big deal out of me working at the farm and running into the barn that night for the horses. He told the court about me sharing that venison at the campground and talked up big how I was the one took care of eight-year-old Andrew Hardesty and jumped into the river to save him, and how that boy had been reunited with his mother. He also pointed out that I was the one who discovered Andrew couldn't read and how I got him some help. He made me think that hey, *really*, if you stood back and took the long view, I wasn't a total screwup!

But then some other lawyer person, a woman, stood and detailed out loud how I stole the truck and caused a bunch of damage, including the burned-out tires and the cab, which was aluminum and had melted. The good news, they said, is that the truck was hauling a load of logs in the trailer, but that the trailer was intact so there was no additional loss there. Still, estimated total damages was fifteen thousand dollars.

It was pretty depressing to hear that final figure. That's the restitution I had to pay back. I figured I could pay it off in about ten years if I got a decent job after high school. That is, if I ever finished high school.

Finally, it was time for the judge—excuse me, the master of the court—to weigh it all up in his head and come up with his wise disposition order for me.

Just when I thought the whole ordeal was about over, something else happened. This guy came forward. He was wearing jeans, but he had a jacket and tie on, like he was halfway dressed for court. He favored one leg as he moved to the front of the courtroom. He said his name was Edward Houseman and told the court he worked for Houseman Freight Company. I didn't recognize him at first, but he was the truck driver I ripped off. The guy with the cell phone pressed to his ear who limped into that restaurant talking about biscuits and sausage gravy. I remembered the sound of his boots on the gravel and the clenched-up feeling in my stomach 'cause I was already thinking of stealing his truck.

So why did *he* show up? So he could take a good look at me and spit in my face for what I done?

I sighed and slumped back in my chair, bracing myself.

"Your Honor," the truck driver began, "I came today for a couple of reasons. Number one, I wanted a good look at the young man who stole my Kenworth back in September."

He turned and had his good look at me and, as much as I wanted to, I did not drop my eyes.

"This young man dealt my business a big wallop. But Your Honor, I am also here because I have heard all the facts about Michael Griswald. I heard how he ran into that barn on fire, and how he jumped into the river to save that little boy. I had a little boy once myself and I can tell you this, that I wished he were here now to help me run my business . . ."

The guy stopped and paused to sort of rub the end of his nose. I wondered if he was stifling a sneeze—or something else.

Then he continued: "What I'd like to do, if the court will allow it, is to make an offer to this young man. If Michael Griswald—Digger, as he is known—can finish his time and go back to high school and graduate without getting into any more trouble, and if he's willing to work for me, the summer after he gets out of juvenile detention, to pay back some of the damages, then I will forgive the rest of the restitution charges, full and complete."

I sat up in the chair and shifted position. My eyes did not leave Mr. Houseman. Was he serious? I glanced at my public defender beside me and saw he had this silly grin on his face.

I leaned toward him. "Is this for real?" I whispered.

He whispered back, "I'll tell you, Digger, truck drivers make good money. You could set yourself up for a full-time job!"

The master of the court asked me to stand.

"Michael Griswald, what do you say to Mr. Houseman? Can you promise to finish your time, return to high school, work one summer for him, and graduate without getting into any more trouble?"

Where was my voice? I took another breath.

"Yes! Yes, sir, Your Honor," I said. Then I turned toward Mr. Houseman. "I'm grateful to you, sir. And I want to say that I am truly sorry for what I did."

Mr. Houseman nodded and kind of lifted his hand. "A long time ago, when I was a boy your age, I got into trouble myself. Someone gave me a second chance, and I made good with it. Except for this bum knee and losing my son, I've had a good life. It's time for me to give back."

I nodded my thanks again to this bighearted man I had wronged and who I didn't even know. This man who was giving me a second chance.

Incredible. A second chance. A chance to really start over. A chance to give back and lead a good life . . .

Was it possible that one day I could make up some—if only a little—for the life I had taken from a three-year-old boy?

At the Deep Valley Juvenile Detention Center, where I started a new, ten-month gig and walked around all day in slippers, I once again had a bed with scratchy blankets in a row with eleven other beds. In between my bed and the next was a tall gray metal locker for my toothbrush and a change of clothes. Only this time, I had something to tape up inside the locker door. I had that picture LeeAnn drew of a rainbow— with me on one side, and home on the other.

ACKNOWLEDGMENTS

I have many people to thank for helping me research this book. First on my list are the teachers, counselors, administrators—and boys—at Backbone Mountain and Meadow Mountain Youth Centers, two juvenile detention centers in western Maryland run by the Maryland State Department of Juvenile Services. Michael Lewis, principal for the youth centers; David Symanski, lead teacher; Mari Freno, mental health counselor; and Barbara Miltenberger, reading specialist, were especially helpful.

I thank Mark Livingston, a therapist at Potomac Ridge School in Crownsville, Maryland, for helping me begin to understand the challenges of treating young people who get in trouble. And I am grateful to Judith Hale, a reading specialist in Frederick County, Maryland, for her special insights.

I appreciate the education in garbage truck operations from Mike Doherty of Waste Management in Columbia, Maryland. And I thank a big rig truck driver, who wishes to remain anonymous, for teaching me how to throw the splitter and drive an eighteen-wheeler. (No one has to worry— I won't be going for my Class B license anytime soon.)

For the information they provided, I thank the U.S. National Park Service, the Maryland Highway Administration, the Maryland State Police, the Maryland State's Attorney's Office, and John McNeece of the Maryland Fire and Rescue Institute in College Park.

To all of the devoted, hardworking people at Days End Farm, a horse rescue facility in Woodbine, Maryland, a big thank you—especially Sue Miller, Pam Wheeler, and Brittney Carow. They are bighearted miracle workers.

Family friend and outdoorsman Bill Lane has my appreciation for his detailed lesson in field dressing a deer. And once again, I thank former Maryland State Senator John Bambacus and his wife, Karen, residents of western Maryland, for their hospitality—and their thoughts.

I wish to acknowledge the information I gleaned from the *U.S. Army Survival Handbook*, revised and updated by Sergeant First Class Matt Larsen; and the charming, readable guide *The C&O Canal Companion*, by Mike High. Hiking or biking on any part of the beautiful, restored canal towpath from Georgetown to Cumberland, Maryland, is a step back in time and an enchanting experience.

Finally, to all the readers of *Red Kayak* who raised their hands, e-mailed, and wrote wanting to know what happened to the boys, I thank you, too, because without your interest and inspiration, I would not have gone back to Digger.

ACKNOWLEDGMENTS

CHAPTER ONE

After all this time, I still ask myself: *Was it my fault?*
Maybe. Maybe not.

Either way, I wonder what would have happened if I'd called out a warning. Or kept my mouth shut later. Would J.T. and Digger still be my best friends? Would the DiAngelos still be living next door?

One thing's for sure: If none of this had happened, I'd be out there crabbing every day, baiting my pots in the morning and pulling them in after school. Fall's a great time for catching crabs before the females head south and the males burrow into the mud. I could fix the engine on the boat easy if I wanted. It's not broken like I told Dad. Probably nothing but some air in the lines from settin' there so long. I could bleed the engine tonight, set my alarm for 4 A.M., and be on the river before the sun was up over the tree line.

Don't think it didn't bother me, the way those traps sat all summer, stacked four deep against the back of Dad's toolshed. Some never even got hosed off, they were stashed in such a hurry. Be a lot of work to clean 'em up and re-zinc them, too, so they don't corrode. In just a few days, though, I could have four rows of twenty-five sunken pots out there, each one marked with a fresh-painted orange buoy, and all one hundred of those pots soaked and baited with razor clams. Afternoons, I could be hauling in crabs hand over fist, and right now, a bushel of big number-one jimmies would fetch me seventy dollars from the whole-saler—maybe even more, since the price of crabs has gone through the roof.

But this is all so complicated. I can't go back out on the water. Not yet anyway. I can't help it; I keep asking myself, *What if this, what if that?* And then in my mind I see that red kayak . . .

My dad says stop thinking that way. "You be lookin' back-ward all the time, Brady, you're gonna have one heck of a crook in the neck." He smiles when he says that. But I know what he means deep down, and it's not funny. You can't keep dwelling on the past when you can't undo it. You can't make it happen any different than it did.

My cousin Carl comes over a lot. He's a paramedic and sees a lot of gross stuff, so he knows about getting things out of your head. "Talk it out there, boy," he keeps telling me. "What? You think you're alone? You think other people don't have these feelings?" But even Carl admits he's never been in quite the same position as me.

Mom has helped a lot, too, although I know it was really hard for her, because of my sister.

Mostly, I wish I could just stop going over it in my mind.

But it replays all the time. Like waves breaking on the narrow beach down at the river. Sometimes, after school, I walk down there to sit on the bank and do nothing. Just let the sun bake my face and listen to those waves hitting the shore, one after the other.

Tilly always follows me and I let her. Tilly's my yellow Lab. She lays down with her head on her paws and knows to leave me alone when I'm thinking. Despite everything, I still marvel at how all those tiny ripples in the water can catch the sunlight and make the river shimmer like a million jewels were strewn on the surface. Deceptive, how other times the same water can seem as smooth as glass. You'd never know that underneath, the currents run so hard and so fast.

It's a pretty river, the Corsica. But it doesn't have a heart . . .

CHAPTER TWO

In some ways, it started over a year ago. But I want to get the worst over first, so I'm going to start with what happened six months ago, in the spring. That morning, we were waiting, my two friends and I, for the ambulance to come, and J.T. took a swig from his bottle of green tea. I remember this because Digger was trying to pick a fight, and it all started with J.T.'s green tea.

No one was hurt—that's not why the ambulance was coming. My cousin Carl had this old ambulance that the county still uses for a backup, and when he had the early shift, he would swing by and give us a ride to school. School's only a couple miles away, but it's a forty-minute ride on that dang bus because we're first pickup on the loop. Besides, it was pretty cool getting a ride in the ambulance.

J.T. almost always waits for the bus with me. He lives next door on his family's chicken farm. A soybean field between my house and his has a path worn down through the middle of it we're back and forth so much. And Digger is across the road, not too far the other way. Sometimes, he walks over to join us—that, or his father will drop him off from his dump truck on his way to a job.

So we were in the driveway that morning, waiting for Carl to pick us up. Backpacks on the ground. Hunched in our parkas because it was chilly. Taking turns throwing the tennis ball for Tilly, who never quits. And Digger snatched the bottle of green tea out of J.T.'s hands and started laughing. "What the—"

"Shhhhh!" I'm always having to tone down Digger. "My mom can hear!" And she can't stand to hear us cuss.

We cast a glance back at the house.

Digger held the bottle up, out of J.T.'s reach. "Green tea with ginseng and *honey?*" He sounded disgusted.

It made me uncomfortable, the way Digger talked to J.T. sometimes. And after all those years we spent growing up together.

But J.T. just laughed. He's pretty easygoing. And he swiped the drink back. "Hey," he said. "It's loaded with antioxidants."

"Anti *who?*" Digger screwed up his face.

"You wait, Digger," J.T. warned him. "You and Brady—especially Brady 'cause he's always out in the sun—you'll be all old and wrinkly by the time you're fifty, and I'll have, like, this perfect skin."

"Yeah, like a baby's ass," Digger retorted.

I wanted to tell him to shut up, but I didn't. I could tell when Digger was in one of his moods.

"You're just jealous," J.T. quipped.

"Of *what?*" Digger demanded.

"Guys!" I called out, stopping everything like a referee's whistle. When they looked at me, I pivoted and flung the ball for Tilly. We watched it land and roll downhill toward our dock. At the same time my father's band saw started up in the old tractor shed, which Dad has transformed into his woodworking shop. Where we live used to be a farm, but it's not anymore. The barn and the farmhouse burned down years ago—before my parents bought the property and built a one-story brick rancher. My dad is a waterman half the year, a boat carpenter the other half, and even though crabbing season started April 1, he'd been working Mondays in the shop because he was making more money building cabinets than crabbing, especially now that crabs were getting scarce.

Last year, the state legislature cut Dad's workday from fourteen hours down to eight. Then the governor took away the month of November, and it hurt us financially. My mom had to put in extra hours at the nursing home, and Dad was pretty ticked off. "They're blamin' the wrong people!" he railed. "Pollution and development—that's what's killin' us. Bay be right smart of crabs if it weren't for all the damned condo-*minions* going up!"

I don't know. We had a little argument about it after a scientist came to school. He said my dad was only half right—about the pollution and all. "We're fishing the bay too hard," that guy kept saying. "Too many crab pots, too many trotlines. You have to take the long look."

When Dad's noisy band saw stopped, I glanced at J.T. and Digger and wondered which way the conversation would go.

"What's your dad working on?" J.T. asked.

"Dr. Finney's sailboat," I said, glad to move off the subject of J.T.'s green tea. "Thirty-foot Seawind ketch. Twenty-five years old—fiberglass hull but a lot of solid wood trim topside."

J.T. arched his eyebrows. "Wow. He's got his work cut out for him."

"He's completely gutting it," I said. "Dr. Finney's going to put in this incredible electronics system. GPS. Flat-screen TV. Security." I knew this would make J.T. drool because he loves all that technical stuff.

But it only made Digger angry. He kicked a rock in the driveway. "Some people got too much money for their own damn good."

When a pair of noisy mallards flew over, we looked up. Even Tilly dropped the ball and started barking. In the west, I noticed dark clouds piling up across the horizon, like a distant mountain range.

"If the weather didn't look so bad, I'd say come on over this afternoon. We could take a little spin down the river." I felt bad for Digger sometimes. On account of his family.

"Can't go," he mumbled, still kicking his toe in the dirt. "I gotta help my old man haul gravel."

"Yeah, me neither," J.T. said. "I erased my entire hard drive last night. I need to load everything back on and rewrite that essay for English. Hey, Brady, remember those oxymorons we talked about in lit the other day?"

"Jumbo shrimp?" I asked.

"Yeah—and *military intelligence*," J.T. reminded me.

I grinned.

"Well, I got a good one for you," J.T. said. *"Microsoft Works."*

Even Digger lifted his head and chuckled. "A *perfect idiot,*" he added.

So there we were, all of us laughing because we'd knocked out four oxymorons smack in a row—and that's when we first saw the red kayak.

From where we stood, you could see down the grassy slope behind our house, on past Dad's shop and the dock, to the creek. And out there, heading our way, was Mr. DiAngelo's new red kayak.

Digger's face lit up. "The Italian stallion," he chortled, a dual reference to the heritage of our new neighbor, Marcellus DiAngelo, and his obsession with physical fitness. Cupping his hands around his mouth, Digger pretended to call out: "Paddle hard, you sucker!"

He and J.T. exchanged this look I didn't quite catch, and J.T. started laughing, too.

But I shook my head. "He shouldn't be going out there today. When he gets down by the point—he'll *fly* down the river." I was sure Mr. DiAngelo didn't know about how the wind picked up once you left our creek and hit the open water. Not to mention the spring tides. Sometimes they were so strong they'd suck the crab-pot buoys under. I doubted whether Mr. DiAngelo knew that; he'd only had the kayak a few weeks.

"Really, guys. We ought to yell something," I said soberly.

J.T. shook his head. "He's too far away. He won't hear you."

"Why should we anyway?" Digger asked with a scowl. "Just

because you baby-sat for their little kid and you're in love with his wife?"

An overstatement if I ever heard one. Although I did take care of their son one afternoon when Mrs. DiAngelo had to go over the bridge to Annapolis for a doctor's appointment. And she is a very good-looking woman—but even J.T. and Digger thought so.

"Ben's cool," I said, trying to make light of it. "We did LEGOs."

J.T. chuckled and looked at his sneakers.

Sneering, Digger stuffed his hands in his pockets. "Look, Brady," he said, "if he's stupid enough to be out there today, he can take what's coming. Besides, he deserves it."

Tilly whined because she was waiting for me to throw the ball again.

"That water is damn cold," I said as I stooped to pick up the ball. It was only the middle of April, and the water temperature probably wasn't even fifty degrees yet. "Exposure, you know? If he fell in, he could die in, like, twenty minutes."

Digger smiled. "Exactly," he said calmly. "We'd all be so lucky."

At that point, I threw the ball so hard it landed in the marsh near the water. Tilly took off after it like a shot and disappeared into the tall grass.

"Come on." I made eye contact with Digger when I said it again: "Let's yell something."

But we didn't.

Digger dropped his eyes and backed off. When he turned in profile, I glimpsed the hard lines of his scowl as he gazed out toward that red kayak. It was the first time I realized how much anger Digger had packed inside. I knew he was sore because the DiAngelos bought his grandfather's farm, tore down the old house, and built a mansion up there on the bluff. But up until then, maybe I hadn't realized how much it bothered him.

Of course it didn't help that we'd all been booted off the property a few days ago. But if you asked me, Mr. DiAngelo was pretty nice about it. He didn't yell, or offend us, or anything like that. He merely asked us to leave because we were trespassing. And Digger *did* have that cigarette lit. I mean, Mr. DiAngelo had a right. For all he knew, we could have started a fire or something.

But from Digger's point of view, we were only hanging out under *our* cliff, where we hung out a million times over the last thirteen years. That cliff and all the property the DiAngelos now own was all part of our stomping grounds. We shot tin cans out on the cornfield. Built forts in the woods. Raced go-carts down the tractor roads. So you know, I *did* feel for some of Digger's frustration.

What I don't understand is how Digger could have been so callous that morning: *If he's stupid enough to be out there, he can take what's coming* . . . How Digger—and J.T., too—could have been so blind to the awful possibilities. Even after I reminded them: *He could die in, like, twenty minutes . . . We ought to yell something* . . .

When, exactly, did they begin to feel shamed by it?

Because it has always shamed me.